A Pressing Affair

A Pressing Affair

ELEANOR KELLEY

atmosphere press

Chapter One

As Kate stepped out of the elevator, she was overwhelmed with memories of her mother's death. Despite being wrapped in a warm cashmere coat and heavy woolen scarf, she felt chilled to the bone. The hospital looked different than when her mom was sick, but the sounds and smells were the same. The beeping, always the beeping, and the smells—bodily fluids, cleaning fluids, disinfecting soap, and recycled air—were otherworldly. So too was the harsh lighting. Kate guessed the bright lights were a necessary evil but wondered if they were just overcompensating for hallways devoid of natural light.

Wishing she could be anywhere else but in this world of the sick and dying, she looked at the scene before her, a bullpen of medical personnel in everything from hospital scrubs to brightly patterned shirts and white coats. Because everyone was wearing clogs, it was getting harder to tell the doctors from the residents, medical students, or nurses. Maybe that was the plan. Passing family members were less likely to ask questions if they weren't sure whom to bother.

Everyone seemed to be working on a computer, looking at someone else's computer, or milling about waiting for an open computer. The days of pen to paper were long gone.

No one took notice of her as she stood frozen in the past. A wave of sadness washed over her as she remembered the ten days that she, her sister, Sue, and their dad had waited for her mom to come back after a grueling ten-hour surgery. Their weeklong vigil, prayers, and chapel visits morphed into Kate bargaining with all the saints and the Almighty. She had promised them she'd be a kinder, better person if her mom got better. It had all seemed to last forever. And then it didn't.

"It's just your mother's time to go home to her family in heaven," Father Joe had told them. *Baloney*, thought Kate. *My mom's family is right here on earth.* Close to saying that and then some, her common sense and Irish Catholic guilt took over.

Her mom had been gone almost three years, but Kate's grief was still raw. It tugged at her heart when she least expected it. Seeing her mom's favorite iced tea in the grocery aisle or hearing a Barry Manilow song on the radio would bring on a deluge of tears. It was, as the poet Maya Angelou said, "the sting of death here in my heart and mind and memories."

Lost in her thoughts, Kate was jolted into the here and now when she heard, "Hi Mom, nice of you to come."

She turned to see her youngest daughter, Jamie, standing next to her. Dressed in striped yoga pants with a neon-pink shirt, Jamie's hair was in a messy bun. Kate was taken aback. Was her daughter on the way to the gym, or coming from the gym? Probably neither. This was acceptable attire for most young women her age. Jamie was no different. Still, Kate wondered what had happened to dressing appropriately. Gone the way of pen and paper, she decided.

Then again, Harry wouldn't care if their children came to the hospital in pajamas. What the Johnson kids wanted, Harry wanted, and he made sure they got it. It was the gospel according to Harry, but it wasn't helping him much now. He may have never met a stain he couldn't handle, but that wasn't true of his heart condition.

Jamie, along with her sister, Anne, and brother, Mark, was on day two of her bedside vigil when Kate arrived. This was Kate's first visit, as it had been over a year since she'd seen, spoken to, or heard from her ex-husband or their three children.

She might not have heard about Harry's condition had he not collapsed on the course playing a round of golf with the bishop.

When someone hit the proverbial dirt next to Bishop George, it made the papers. She'd seen the story on page two, top right-hand side, with a picture of George walking off the course. Didn't get much better than that. Harry would love the up-front placement and being with the bishop was a spiritual bonus.

Harry was head of the parish council, and Kate was PTA chairwoman and distributed communion. Sunday mass was a family affair, and all three children had been altar servers. They all had attended Catholic elementary schools, high schools, and colleges. A close friend to their parish priests and an even better friend to the bishop,

Harry had been proud to say he cleaned church vestments free of charge. He also made it a point to take the parish priests—without Kate—to dinner at least once a month. More often than not, it was to one of three restaurants he frequented, as he liked being called by name and having his cocktail waiting for him. Kate nearly laughed out loud at the irony. The medical cocktails he was getting now were a far cry from his vodka and tonic with a lot of ice and two limes.

Kate was thinking she could use a cocktail. It wouldn't be an easy visit. Nevertheless, she moved forward as Jamie approached her, saying curtly, "Follow me; I'll show you to his room."

"Is he doing okay?"

"How do you think he's doing?" Jamie spat out. "He's had a major stroke and the doctors think he'll probably have another one. He can't speak, barely opens his eyes, and can't move his arms and legs. I'd say he is far from okay!"

Momentarily speechless at her daughter's angry response, Kate's thoughts catapulted back to the brutal divorce. If Jamie's response was an indicator of how the other two children felt, this visit could be more painful than their actual breakup.

She brushed off Jamie's harsh words and quietly asked, "Think I shouldn't go in?"

Before Jamie answered, Mark came out of Harry's room, his wife Carla beside him. Kate was surprised to see Carla, as she and Harry were not always on the best terms. Harry had made it clear, five years ago on their wedding day, that Mark could have done better than Carla and had often referred to her as "Mark's hillbilly wife." Though

Carla was from the southern part of the state, and her upbringing had been modest, Kate was sure the family had never sweated it out in a non-air-conditioned doublewide.

Carla didn't think much of Harry either and often "joked" that he was obviously a victim of believing his own press releases. Although not openly hostile to one another, they often butted heads. Kate always said a prayer when they got through a family function without an argument.

Lucky for Kate, she was spared any conversation, as Carla gave her a quick once-over and walked right by, head held high. Mark stopped momentarily and gave Kate a snappy, "Seeing as you're here now, Mother, of course you can come in. Just don't upset him."

Aha, she thought, *Harry isn't in the room dying after all; he's standing right in front of me.* Mark was Harry's clone. His "Don't upset him" phrase was gender replacement for Harry's "Don't upset your mother" mantra.

Surprised at how quickly bad memories resurfaced, she turned her attention to her son. Dressed in a cream-colored cashmere sweater, camel-colored pants, and tasseled loafers, Mark was a Harry look-alike. His hair was darker, and he was a few inches taller, but he emitted the same verbal and physical swagger as his father. Her assessment complete, Kate smiled and answered, "Of course, I would never want to upset your father."

Mark had always been a sassy child, and that obviously hadn't changed. Harry referred to it as spunk and moxie. Kate referred to it as bad behavior. But still, she felt a deep love for him. She ached for him and for her other two children. That ache felt like a phantom connection that had remained long after they cut her out of their lives.

Chapter Two

The ear-splitting noise was enough to wake the dead. Maybe he was dead, and the loud clanging had brought him back among the living. He opened his eyes and saw nothing but total darkness. Blinking a few times, he hoped his vision would return, but that hadn't happened.

Harry had no idea how he had gotten to where he was, or even if he was still on earth. Was this purgatory? Nah, he remembered Bishop George saying all the years of prayers for the poor souls lingering there had cleaned the place out.

Don't think it's heaven because it's way too dark, and I don't hear any soft music or welcoming words from St. Peter. Can't be hell, he decided. *Done way too much good to burn in the fires of the damned. I'm sounding like a third-grade catechism book. Still have a memory—good sign.*

A sigh of recognition and relief curled around his throat before escaping through his half-open mouth, fixed in a self-congratulatory smile. He knew he was lying on some sort of flat, relatively comfortable surface, as his back and neck weren't aching.

All I need to do is get up. Get moving.

But his legs were frozen in place. When he tried to move his arms, they were as immobile as his legs.

Must be tied down. Maybe I've been kidnapped and I'm being held for ransom. Wonder how much I'd be worth? Think John Paul Getty III had a $17 million ransom. They cut off his ear to make the grandfather pay. Hate to lose an ear or even a finger. Need to get out of here. Am I in some cold, dark cellar?

But as he was comfortably warm and didn't detect any dank odors associated with cold cellars, he immediately ruled that out. He tried sitting up but failed at that, too.

I've been drugged and they've immobilized me. Probably one of those roofie things that can end up in your drink at a bar. Wait—no, it can't be. They make people loopy; I'm clear-headed. Am I buried alive?

Terrified at the thought, he began to panic. His breath exploded in fast, short bursts; his pulse quickened. How long would it be before he ran out of air? He had to get out before it was too late.

Opening his mouth to call for help, he heard a low, grinding noise on his right side. No—more of a buzzing or beeping, maybe some sort of machine. It was getting louder. He picked up what he thought might be people talking. Trying to sort it all out, his eyes were suddenly hit with a blinding light.

Dear God, he thought. *I'm heading to the light—to the big dry-cleaning emporium in the sky.*

Harry's ascension, into what he presumed was heaven, was interrupted by two blurry figures talking over him.

"EMTs said he collapsed on the fourteenth green. Said he'd been golfing with the bishop. The bishop called 911. Think he gave him CPR while they waited for the ambulance?"

"Haven't a clue. Hope he added last rites between compressions. It was a close call. He's lucky they got him here in time."

"You know, he's that dry-cleaning guy from TV—the one in the ad for Press Agents."

"No kidding? Too bad he can't take care of his own pressing needs."

"Sick. Be careful what you say, his eyes have opened a few times. He might be able to hear us and from what I've heard, he could be brutal to his workers."

Harry Johnson was fifty-nine years old, good-looking, charming, and a dry-cleaning dynamo. He owned twenty-five Press Agents dry-cleaning stores, a fleet of pick-up and delivery vans, and his own office building. He also had a boatload of commercial dry-cleaning contracts and hundreds of customers swearing their lives were better because of the "Press Agents crease."

Judging from the bits of bedside conversation he heard, Harry began to think he'd had some sort of incident. He had no memory of what had happened, nor how he had gotten to what he now presumed was a medical facility. When he tried to focus on his surroundings, all he saw were gray fuzzy shapes.

He knew he was alive, so his panic subsided. But he wondered what had taken him to the brink of life everlasting.

He heard something about the bishop, but he couldn't make out the rest. Had Bishop George given him last rites? That made sense; he and George had gone to elementary and high school together. When Harry went off to college, George joined the seminary. When Harry married Kate, Father George officiated at the ceremony. George was a like a member of the family, and Harry trusted him more than his own brother.

With similar can-do attitudes and will-do determination, the two men were leaders in their fields. For Harry, it was the dry-cleaning business; for Bishop George, it was the hierarchy of the Catholic Church.

George had baptized Kate and Harry's three children and was included in many family functions. The two men shared a love of golf, fine wine, and upscale dining. They also shared secrets of the past. Harry wondered if that had something to do with his current state. Had something about their high school years surfaced? Did George betray him? He hoped not, but he had a nagging feeling something wasn't right between him and his childhood friend.

As Harry struggled, trying to remember what part Bishop George could have played in his current state, a picture of him and George hazily came into focus.

We were on the golf course waiting for the foursome in front of us to move on. Bunch of old guys playing slow as the itch. The thirteenth or fourteenth green, I think. Blazing sun. Hot and humid. We were laughing over one of George's corny Irish jokes told in his awful brogue.

The jokes weren't that funny, but George's Irish brogue was. Though George wasn't a bit Irish, after a trip to Ireland with Kate and Harry, he was infused with the gift of gab and a bit of the blarney.

What were we gabbing about when I went down? Was George beating me? Were we betting who'd make par? Hope he didn't best me.

Harry hated to lose and was comfortable miscounting strokes to keep it from happening. It might not have been the wisest of moves when playing with someone who saved souls for a living, but Harry was saving face. That counted for more than a few missed strokes between friends.

I took the top off a bottle of water, took a few gulps...and then what?

Trying to remember anything more about the day left Harry thinking only about the cold bottle of water. Why couldn't he remember more? What if his memory lapses were permanent?

As daunting as that would be, he decided it was more important that he try to communicate with someone. He attempted to say something, but no sound came out. Then he heard a voice that sounded familiar, but he couldn't put a face to it.

"The doctors say he should eventually come out of this. Even though he can't speak, he can probably hear us," his son, Mark, said. "He's opened his eyes a few times, but when I asked him how he was feeling, he just closed his eyes again."

"So, like, what do we do?" Carla asked. "Keep talking to him? Bring some CDs and play his favorite music? I read that some guy in a coma woke up thinking he was Elvis because they played his favorite Elvis music when he was out. When he got over the fact that he wasn't the king of rock-and-roll, he became an Elvis impersonator."

"Stop with the Elvis talk!" Mark bellowed, as Harry panicked.

Thank God you shut her up. If Carla's here, this is worse than I imagined. She's probably got a laundry list of what she'll buy if this all goes south. Hope that little hillbilly wife of his isn't thinking of helping me along with a quick flip of a switch.

But hillbilly or not, he needed her and Mark. Someone needed to clear things up. His eyes couldn't focus, and he couldn't process an entire conversation. When he tried to speak, no words came out. When he tried to raise his hand, he could move only his index finger. He wasn't sure that had even moved.

As he drifted in and out of consciousness, Harry tried to make sense of what had happened on the golf course. In the midst of it all he heard another familiar voice. His daughter Anne? Harry woozily assumed she must be in his room.

Thank goodness she's here. She'll get me out of this place. Hope she's left her loser husband Joe home. Listening to him is coma-inducing in itself. Why the hell did she marry him anyway?

Moments later he heard Anne blurt out, "When Father George called yesterday, I thought it was another one of his jokes. We couldn't get a flight home till this morning. Can't believe this is happening. Was it another stroke? Worse than last time?"

"Slow down. Take a breath, they assume it's a stroke, but they are still doing some tests. He seems to be pretty much the same as yesterday when they brought him," Mark said, exasperated. "We've only been here a half hour or so ourselves. Haven't seen the doc today. The nurse says he's in surgery. He'll be down when he's through. The only thing I know is that Dad's stable."

"Isn't there someone else we can call? What about his cardiologist?"

"Already asked the nurse to contact him. In the meantime, we sit and wait."

And what happens to me in the meantime? I can hardly see, I can barely move, and I can't talk. Why isn't someone doing something? When Kate's sister had that incident, they gave her blood thinners. Came out of it okay. Have they tried that?

Filled with dread and *poor me* thoughts, Harry was confident he'd done nothing to deserve this.

Was it that lazy waitress at the club who never got my drink right and always mixed up my meal? So stupid. Couldn't have been the first one to let her know. Too bad she couldn't take it. Glad she quit. Weeks ago. Probably wasn't her.

Moving on, Harry honed in on his employees. A week or so ago, he'd given a young blonde a good tongue-lashing when his shirts had too little starch. The next time, she overdid it and he got a neck rash. He was furious and wanted to fire her. Since they were short on staff, he settled for docking her a week's pay. She'd cried and complained to her store manager. A week later, she'd quit.

Did she put toxic chemicals in my shirts? Possible. She handles all sorts of cleaning fluids. Didn't notice they had an odd odor—but I did start having stomach problems.

As he mulled over poisoning by toxic shirt, he had a sudden revelation. His ex-wife, Kate, was a chemist!

She's crazy enough. Blamed me for her estrangement from the kids. Could have mixed up a poison concoction.

Hired someone to slip it in my drink or in the water bottle at the course. Happened to Jane Stanford, who founded the university. Her secretary added a little strychnine to her mineral water. Last drink she ever took. Socrates drank poison tea—but think that was hemlock. Not sure hemlock's easy to get.

If Kate had put something in his water bottle, Harry thought as he drifted off, someone had helped her. George?

Chapter Three

Unable to figure out whether it was the next hour, the next day, or the next week, Harry was sure of one thing: his vision was clearing. He was able to see machines on one side of his bed and two empty chairs on the other.

Must be moving my head. Things are looking up. What else is working? Should ring the nurse.

Seeing the call button clipped to his pillow, he tried to reach for it. His arm refused to move. A bit of a setback, but nothing he believed wouldn't eventually solve itself. He knew, or thought he knew, his fingers could move. Maybe his toes could do the same. Willing himself to move, he heard the faint rustling of the sheets at the end of his bed.

Toes can move too. If fingers, toes, and head can move, good sign. Matter of time till I'm out of here.

Happy his vision was improving and he had movement, he was shocked to hear his children were still in the room.

Didn't hear them seconds ago. Must have drifted off.

Trying to sort it all out, he heard his brother, Steve.

"Didn't believe it when George told me. Harry and I had lunch just last week. He seemed fine. Was his usual self, shaking hands with everybody in the restaurant. They really think it's another stroke?"

As Harry's eyes fluttered open, Steve added, "Looks like he can see us. Think he knows where he's at?"

Course I can see you. Not dead yet! If I had died, you could afford to send your boys to that fancy school. Buy your wife decent-looking clothes.

With Steve having joined the fray, Harry wondered if he had had something to do with his stroke. Steve insisted they have a beer with their burgers at lunch. He might have slipped something into the beer when Harry was in the bathroom.

If incapacitated any longer, Steve might try to take over running the business. Wouldn't sit well with Anne and Mark. Think that's in my will. Even have a will? Harry thought as he fell back to sleep.

When he woke up again, Harry's thoughts flipped to his youngest daughter, Jamie.

Where's Jamie? Remember someone talking about yoga class. Maybe Jamie. Only one into that yin and yang mumbo jumbo.

Harry thought it all foolish nonsense. Kate attributed it to Jamie being their artsy child who looked at the world from a different perspective. Harry only cared about the right Press Agents perspectives in their ads. Jamie was interning at Press Agents, working on advertising and promotions.

It had been Jamie's idea to add television advertising

and bus cards. Her prompting got Harry in front of the TV cameras extolling the virtues of "Our family taking care of your family's pressing need."

Kate said it was hokey. Better off hiring a professional. So wrong. Bet Kate isn't so smug now. Twenty-five locations. Doubled since she abandoned us.

Happy to have proved Kate wrong yet again, he drifted into a deep sleep, a smile slowly spreading across his face.

Chapter Four

Like other things in their less-than-perfect union, how the relationship had begun depended on who was walking back in time. Kate said she'd noticed the good-looking Harry on campus but had never spoken to him until he came into the coffee shop one day. Harry said he'd never noticed Kate and was interested only in flirting with her at the coffee shop. One thing rang true in both recollections: the campus coffee shop was where they had met, and the Lincoln penny had brought them together.

Kate O'Brien was a sophomore chemistry student with shoulder-length, wavy red hair, fair-freckled skin, green eyes, and thin lips. Her mother thought she looked like the Irish actress Maureen O'Hara. Kate didn't see the resemblance, but never minded being compared to a woman known for her strong-willed, fiery roles. O'Hara was from the same county outside Dublin as Kate's great-grandparents, and Kate shared her same August birthday, which also factored in.

On that particular Friday afternoon, Kate and her chemistry notes were sitting at a small window table at the St. Francis campus coffee house. It was twenty-five degrees outside and snowing. Attempting to memorize the mnemonic for the amino acids, she lost her focus when she saw two kids playing in the park across the street. Dressed in full blizzard gear of one-piece snowsuits, alpine flapjack hats, black boots, and multicolored mittens, they were rolling small balls of packed snow through the fresh powder—but there wasn't enough snow yet and it wasn't good for packing. Seeing two more kids join in, Kate knew that reinforcements wouldn't help.

She watched the four boys come together in a small circle. They appeared to be assessing the situation. Suddenly, they all ran away in different directions and flung themselves in the snow, flapping their arms like chickens. Plans had changed.

I made the best snow angels, Kate recalled, smiling. *My sister Sue couldn't come close. She'd ruin hers when she stood up. I had the getting up part down; never used my hands or arms. Bet I can still do her one better.*

Turning away from the snow angels, back to her open notebook, she scanned the page for her amino acid notes. She read them over once, then, frustrated, closed the notebook and reached for her latte.

Oblivious to the people around her, Kate didn't see Harry heading to her table.

"A penny for your thoughts," he said, dropping a shiny Lincoln penny on her table.

She looked down at the penny, then up at Harry, and countered with, "Really? That's the best you got?"

Harry smiled, reached into his pocket to pull out

another Lincoln, and said, "How 'bout I double down?"

"Thanks for giving me your two cents," she said, flipping the coins as she turned the page in her notebook.

Undaunted by her lack of attention, Harry unbuttoned his coat, shook the snow from his hair, and sat down, "I'm Harry Johnson."

Kate held back a giggle, took a sip of her latte, and grinned.

In a blue crewneck sweater over a green checked shirt and well-worn khakis, Harry was casually handsome. His sandy-colored, wavy hair needed a comb, a cut, or both, but it suited him. He had a wide smile and perfect white teeth. Harry had a style entirely his own, and looking up into his blue eyes, Kate felt overwhelmed. She believed she was just average-looking and was surprised this Harry guy had given her a second look.

Should have combed my hair after I took off my hat. Shouldn't have worn my old sweater. It's too big. Looks like I belong on the street pushing a shopping cart, not sipping coffee in this trendy place. Why didn't I put on some mascara and lip gloss? He looks like he stepped out of a fashion shoot.

Exhausted after her quick bout with self-doubt, Kate took a breath. Before she could think of what to say next, Harry was chatting away. In mere minutes he told her he lived in a house off campus with five other guys, had played on the rugby team until he tore his meniscus, and was treasurer of his fraternity. A business major graduating in June, he planned on moving back to Bensenville to live at home and start some sort of laundry pickup and delivery service. His uncle was donating his old van that needed some detailing work on the inside. He also needed to paint over the orange and red "Pete's Plumbing, where a flush beats a full house."

Kate was about to laugh at the slogan when Harry added, "Did you know *U.S. News and World Report* reported that dry cleaning is one of ten fields that aren't glamorous but make people millionaires? It's a cash-and-carry business and has a low failure rate."

Then, revving up, he continued, "I plan to start out small but eventually have a storefront dry-cleaning business. It'll be the only place to go for all your dry-cleaning needs."

There's a real claim to fame, she thought. Harry obviously had visions of dry-cleaning dominance dancing in his head, but why? *What makes someone loony over laundry?* she wondered.

Before she could ask, Harry cut in with, "I also plan to make it environmentally friendly, because that's the way the country is going. Can you even imagine that it was a maid in the 1800s knocking a kerosene lamp over on a tablecloth who started modern-day dry cleaning? The cloth got so clean that kerosene became the cleaning agent used until the 1920s."

Harry paused, and, impressed by his own knowledge, was ready to receive Kate's impression.

"Hmm...and it was an English chemist named Michael Faraday who discovered that tetrachloroethylene could replace the kerosene. It's still the primary cleaning solvent used by dry cleaners worldwide. And I'm Kate, by the way," she added as she pushed her hair back behind her ears.

"Right. I'm impressed. I guess you really know your stuff," Harry said with a large smile and a raised eyebrow.

"Depends on the stuff. I know I now have two Lincoln pennies, the only coins where the portrait faces the right. Penny heads weigh more than tails, making it more common to find a penny facedown. Might keep that in mind if you're looking for a lucky heads-up penny." Kate paused, wondering why she was rattling off useless penny facts.

Harry looked momentarily stunned and confused but quickly countered with, "So I'm not up on penny facts but I do know there's a great table for dinner at the Chop House on the river. I'd feel lucky, pennies aside, if you'd join me tonight for dinner."

His jokes were corny, and he was close to the edge in dry-cleaning fanaticism, but who didn't like a good steak? And at twenty, good looks and sex appeal took precedent over less-than-stimulating conversation.

"Nothing like a good tenderloin to turn a girl's head," she replied.

Chapter Five

Turn her head he did, and when he asked her out the following night, she immediately called her mother.

"You won't believe it, but one of the cutest, funniest, and most popular guys on campus took me out to dinner last night. He's such a nice guy and so easy to talk to. We laughed a lot and the night seemed to fly by. He asked me out again for tonight. I can't believe it."

"Katie O'Brien, why wouldn't you believe it? You are a good-looking, smart Irish gal, and he's lucky to be dating you. I'll hear no more of that talk. Go out and get yourself a new blouse or sweater. It might give you an ego boost. And for the love of God, put on some lipstick."

It was a typical response from her mom, and Kate loved her for it. She also did as she was told. That evening she wore a new sweater and blouse and didn't forget the lipstick.

After a movie and ice cream, Harry drove Kate back to her dorm. When they pulled up and parked, he quickly hopped out of the car to open her door. She was impressed with his good manners and found herself wondering how she got so lucky to be on a second date with Harry Johnson. He was a campus heartthrob, and he'd asked her out. As they walked up to the dorm his hand brushed her back and her heart did a little summersault. He didn't try to kiss her; just said he had a great time and wished her goodnight.

When she got back to her room she started gushing about Harry and how she had the greatest night of her life. Her roommate, Molly, smiled and listened patiently.

Molly, an Irish girl from Wisconsin, was Kate's freshman suitemate and now sophomore roommate. She had short dark hair, pale Celtic skin, and dark brown eyes. She was an inch and a half over five feet tall on a good day, and on a bad day she'd swear she puffed up an inch. But with a dry sense of humor and deep hearty laugh, she rarely had a bad day. She loved a good joke and never forgot a punchline.

An accomplished Irish dancer, she had numerous first-place ribbons from Feis in Wisconsin and Illinois. That being said, she was never more than a beer away from doing a jig. Kate found it endearing and entertaining and part of what made being Molly's friend an adventure.

Kate trusted Molly's opinion and was anxious to get her reaction to her second date. Molly didn't disappoint.

"So happy for you, Kate. Sounds like the man of your dreams. But, be careful, he might be a dog in sheep's clothing."

"You mean the wolf in sheep's clothing," Kate said, laughing.

"No, I'm confident Aesop's fable says a dog, not a wolf. Either way, that wolf can be a dog," Molly said with a small grin.

Ignoring Molly's warning, Kate rambled on. "Do you think he had a good time? Think he'll ask me out again? What if he hooks up with some hot girl over Christmas break?"

"Enjoy the ride. My brother Michael's in the same fraternity; he said Harry's never dated the same girl for more than a weekend. If you make it more than two, you'll be 'the leader of the pack,'" Molly sang out.

"The Shangri-Las," Kate said, jumping right into their game of quoting infamous tag lines and song lyrics. Molly and Kate had started the competition as freshmen and continued to hone their song game skills.

Most weekday mornings Kate saw Harry on her way to class as he was getting out of his silver Mustang. With its black convertible top and gray leather interior, it was the kind of car Kate's mother would say was "snappy." As clean and shiny as the day it left the showroom, the convertible was Harry's claim to college fame. He always parked in the row closest to the busy student center to give him and his car maximum exposure.

Kate's friends said the car was showy. Kate didn't care, it was part of what made him Harry. She loved it, almost as much as she loved being with him.

As they continued to see each other and weekend dates stretched into weeknight get togethers at the campus bar, Harry's friends were surprised.

"Hard to believe it's the same Harry I've known for four years," Molly's brother Mike said one night over beers. Harry was up at the bar getting popcorn and a pitcher of beer. Molly was about to reply when Kate cut in with a sharp, "What do you mean 'the same Harry?'"

Mike's eyes darted to Molly for help and, sensing he needed a life preserver, she said, "Ha! Kate's not the same either. We're taking Mary's rusted-out beater to buy a twelve-pack of no-name beer while she's riding around in fine Corinthian leather buying the 'champagne of bottled beers.'"

"Not true," Kate said as she put down her glass. I'm a Guinness girl, not a Miller High Lifer."

"That's what you say, but I've seen you sip a few."

"Wrong again. I've never been a sipper, and that, my Irish friend, is an insult to our heritage. My gran says beer bottles have narrow necks to keep the Irish from emptying them in one swig."

Molly laughed. "Ah, luck of the Irish."

Chapter Six

As the end of the school year drew closer, Kate began worrying about what would happen between her and Harry over the summer. Thinking he wouldn't have any free time while starting a new business, she was surprised to hear him tell his fraternity brother Billy he would be working part time at the campus bar in the fall.

"Know I'll need some start-up money, and this seemed like a good way to get some cash and still see guys in the fraternity," Harry said.

Kate, waiting to hear him add, "And Kate's here too," was disappointed when Harry said nothing more. Her disappointment was short-lived when Harry turned to her and said, "My parents are taking me to this new steakhouse the night before graduation, and knowing how you like a good piece of meat, I thought you might want to join us."

"That sounds great. I'd love to meet your family," said Kate, trying to remain calm, but not quite able to mask her feelings of pleasure and relief.

"I'm not sure if any or all of my brothers will come, but having both my parents there will be enough. They've been separated for the last six months, as," Harry continued in a softer voice, "my dad's been having an affair with his paralegal." He looked down. "It's lot to take in, especially for my mom."

"I'm so sorry, Harry. Can't even imagine how tough that must be for you."

"My mom's a circuit court judge and my dad's an attorney, so his little fling is the talk of the court. He's such an ass. Can't believe he would do this to our family. We've barely spoken, but he insists we all play nice and have dinner before graduation.

Not sure what to say, Kate took Harry's hand, and as he looked up, he said, "That's the reason I haven't said much about my family. Don't know why my dad, a successful attorney in a big law firm, would stoop to bonking his paralegal. What was he thinking? He had to know my mom would find out. It's so embarrassing. Our family had a great life and he had to go and ruin it."

"Maybe the separation will make him see what he has to lose. Does the woman still work at his firm?" Kate asked.

"According to my mom, the woman—who's married, by the way—left a few weeks ago. Whether he's still seeing her is anyone's guess. I wonder if Mr. Catholic is still going to mass and communion? What he did is a mortal sin, and he can't argue his way out of this one."

If Kate remembered second-grade catechism correctly, the seventh commandment forbid adultery. She wasn't sure if there were second chances in the mortal sin world, or if it was one shot and eternity with the devil. Maybe a sincere confession could wipe the slate clean. It wasn't something Kate had thought much about, as her own parents had a solid history.

Kate's mom, Betty, and her dad, Ed, had met in third grade when, according to Betty, "He pushed me in the bushes on the way home from school." In her dad's version, her mom was so taken with him, she fell into the bushes trying to walk next to him. Both her parents had attended the same Catholic grade school in their close-knit Irish neighborhood. After high school, her dad served in the Second World War and survived numerous missions as a bomber rear gunner, and her mom went to work in a bank. The year after the war ended, they married, and her father was off to engineering school.

"My mom didn't go to college because my dad was going to engineering school, and two tuitions were too much. She'd gone to high school on a full scholarship, so I'm sure she would have been a great college student," Kate told Molly when they were talking about their families one day. "And," Kate added with a laugh, "she used the money her parents had saved for tuition on a fur coat."

She paused for a moment, as if she were considering her mother's situation for the first time, then blithely went on. "I don't think she felt cheated, but she made it clear my sister and I were expected to graduate from college."

"Sounds like true love. Wonder if Harry would give up his dry-cleaning dreams if you wanted to start your own business."

Not sure how to answer, Kate straightened the books on her desk and said nothing.

"No wonder his dad's involved with another woman," Kate told her mom after dinner with Harry's parents.

"She's a miserable person. I only spent two hours with her, and that was an hour and fifty-five minutes too much. I don't know how they take it. She's exhausting."

"You shouldn't be so judgmental, Katie. Her husband cheated on her. She's suffering," her mom reminded her.

"She's making everyone else suffer too. The restaurant was in a restored Victorian mansion and was too dark. Our table, near a big picture window, was in a draft. Her drink came with onions instead of olives, the butter was too hard, and the rolls weren't warm. Anchovies on her Caesar salad made that inedible, and her fish wasn't worth eating because it was 'utterly' tasteless. She's like a two-year-old. I'm surprised she didn't take her ball and go home."

"What did Harry and his dad say?"

"Nothing. They acted like this was a normal dinner. They didn't seem to be uncomfortable, but I was a wreck. I wasn't sure I'd make it. Didn't want to say the wrong thing and have her come down on me like she had on the fish!"

"Hard to believe you were at a loss for words."

"She did most of the talking, which was good, because Harry and his father are at odds. Lucky for us she didn't get into that. She was nice to me, but I kept waiting for the other shoe to drop."

"Waiting for the other shoe to drop is a way of life for the Irish. I read that it came from late-nineteenth-century tenement living where you could hear the person living above you drop one shoe and you expected the other to follow."

"Thanks for the history lesson, Mom. I hope history doesn't repeat itself at another dinner."

"Welcome to Harry's family," her mom said, laughing.

Chapter Seven

Three months after graduation Harry launched a six-day-a-week dry-cleaning pickup and delivery service out of his uncle's old van. Even with a cleaned-up interior and exterior paint job, the van was not the ideal business vehicle. Sometimes it wouldn't start and other times it wouldn't turn off. Not willing to put additional money into what might be his first bad investment, Harry struggled with the temperamental vehicle and kept plugging away looking for new customers.

Transporting other dry-cleaning companies' work was profitable, but being a one-man show in a run-down plumber's van was only going to take him so far.

"It's going okay, but I'm ready to expand into owning my own store," Harry told Kate.

"You've only been at it a few months; maybe you're jumping the gun. Give it a little more time," Kate suggested.

"I don't need more time, and I don't expect you to

understand. I know this is the right time," Harry said with a twinge of irritation.

How can I understand when you never explain things? Kate said to herself. To Harry she said, "Sorry, sure, you're right."

"Thanks, Kate, appreciate your support," Harry said as he leaned over to kiss her.

The next day Harry began visiting local dry-cleaning stores asking owners about equipment costs, cleaning agents, and solvents for treating stains.

Kate, back at St. Francis for junior year, was impressed with Harry's dedication to growing his business, but as she told Molly, "His dry-cleaning dribble is too much. If he isn't talking about the latest stain remover or the best pressing machine, he's giving me detailed descriptions of every store ripe for purchase."

"Do you hear yourself? What girl wouldn't want to date the future king of the dry-cleaning world? You'll be the queen, and the world of dirty laundry your kingdom," Molly said, laughing at her own joke.

"In other words, I'll be on top of the world looking down on Harry's creation."

"The Carpenters. 'Top of the World.' You'll have to do better than that to beat me. But maybe you're comfortable being in second place, or second string or second fiddle."

"I am second to none in this or any other game. I am the undefeated champion of O'Brien family card games and detective extraordinaire in board games," Kate proudly declared.

Heading out the door to meet Harry, she turned to

Molly and added, "I think I'll make a great queen!"

If Kate was bothered by Molly's ribbing—or by her own boredom with Harry's business—that wasn't what she was thinking about as she walked down the stairs. She felt like royalty when she was with him. Not like Cinderella, queen of the laundry pile, but Kate O'Brien, the girl Harry had chosen, over the most beautiful girls at St. Francis.

That night Harry told Kate he'd put a bid on an underperforming dry-cleaning store not far from St. Francis.

"I think the owner will accept it because he's been trying to sell for the last year or two. It needs a good deep cleaning and some updating, but the pressing machines are in good shape."

Kate smiled, and before she could ask about the financing, Harry added, "My brothers are going to do basic things like cleaning, ripping down wallpaper, and painting, but I'll need an electrician and someone to revamp the exhaust system. My dad called and offered me a loan, so I might as well take advantage of it. He's probably doing it out of guilt, but that's okay with me. It's the least he could do after what he's put us through. All I need is the owner to sign a contract."

Kate was glad Harry would accept his father's offer, and she hoped it signaled a change in his attitude. Might be the beginning of forgiving his father for his indiscretions. If his dad was sorry and willing to make changes, hating him would only hurt Harry because, as Kate's mom often had said, "Hate corrodes the vessel it's carried in."

The owner accepted Harry's price, and his brothers went to work. His uncle's friends did the electrical and exhaust work for cost. Harry's younger brother, Steve, became store manager, Kate hired the counter staff, and the first official Press Agents store was open for business.

Chapter Eight

Press Agents was showing a handsome profit in six months, and Harry was back on the expansion track. He found another struggling store looking to sell and, with Steve's help, convinced the owner to accept their offer and remain as store manager.

"By keeping the owner on, Steve can go between both stores without a problem," he told Kate over dinner. "The owner was happy to have time to tell his customers he was retiring. He said his customers are like his family. 'Our family is dedicated to serving your family's dry-cleaning needs.' Perfect slogan for Press Agents, don't you think?"

"Yeah, yeah, I do," Kate slowly answered. "I like the family bit, think people will relate to that. Good choice. And I was wondering if you think it's a good idea for me to finish school a semester early. If I graduate in December, I'd get a jump on everybody else looking for a job in the spring."

"Yeah, whatever, okay," Harry said as he shook his

head and focused on cutting his meat. Two bites later, he tacked on, "I'm going to run some newspaper ads for this second location offering monthly cleaning deals. You know," he said, putting down his knife, "something like, 'Bring in one sweater and get a pair of pants cleaned for free.' What do you think?" He pointed his fork at Kate.

What Kate thought was that Harry had a hearing problem. He didn't hear a word she had said. Kate pushed it aside, knowing how important Harry's work was to him and should be to her. She smiled sweetly. "Whatever you decide will be best."

Smiling back, Harry said, "Thanks, Kate, that means a lot to me. You mean a lot to me."

As she pushed her potatoes around on her plate and speared her last asparagus. Harry reached across the table to take her hand. She set down her fork and reached for his hand. When their fingers intertwined, a tingle of desire rushed through her, and she blushed. He really was so kind and sweet, and she was upset at herself for being upset with him.

"Just relax. Why don't you and Molly go have a few beers tonight? Play your goofy 'name that tune' game?"

"Goofy is a Walt Disney cartoon character introduced in 1932 as Dippy Dawg. Our game is not goofy."

"You're probably right," Harry said, laughing.

Kate finished up junior year and, after completing all her course requirements, graduated in December. By mid-January she landed a job with a pharmaceutical company.

"We celebrated by going back to the Chop House and splitting chateaubriand and a bottle of rosé just like we did on out first date," Kate told her sister, Sue, when Sue called to congratulate her.

"It was such a wonderful night. I remember being so nervous. So worried I'd say something stupid or have something stuck in my teeth. I made it through and here we are still together over three years later."

"That Harry is a quite a guy. I don't think Pete even remembers where we went on our first date."

"You said it was a disaster. Didn't he spill a drink on you at some bar?"

"No, on the guy I was with, Preston, a real hothead. Bar was crowded and he got bumped. Preston's beer spilled and he turned to throw at punch at Pete. Pete ducked and he hit the bartender. Preston got thrown out, but I stayed to finish my beer. Pete and I started talking. And that was that."

"That Pete knows how to get a girl."

"Best day of his life," Sue shot back.

Kate thought the same about her own life since she'd met Harry. Most of her friends weren't even dating, and she had fallen in love with a kind, good-looking businessman. She couldn't imagine life without him, and she often wondered if they would make a life together. They'd never really spoken much of marriage, but she believed he loved her almost as much as she loved him. And, according to him, he had fallen in love with her, "right after our first date." Hard to believe, after years of always wanting a boyfriend in high school she'd landed the best of the best in college.

Two weeks later, as Harry walked Kate back to the dorm after a Saturday football game, he casually asked her to marry him. His proposal came in the middle of telling her his business was doing well and he thought it was time.

"Time for what?" she said as she stopped to pick up a penny on the sidewalk. Harry smiled as he took another penny from his pocket.

"Doubling down again, Kate. Think it is time we planned a future together."

It wasn't the most romantic of proposals, but Kate didn't mind. After a quick "yes, yes, of course yes," she threw her arms around him. *Life just gets better and better*, she thought.

Not willing to ask his father for engagement ring money, no diamond accompanied his proposal. "I'll get a beautiful ring someday," Harry promised. Kate didn't care; she was happy and madly in love, and believing the Irish proverb, "There is no cure for love but marriage," she was ready to become Mrs. Johnson.

Kate had wanted to call her parents immediately and tell them the news, but Harry insisted he tell his parents first.

"My mom's been through a lot, and my dad's talking about moving back in. After I let her and my dad know, you can call anybody you want."

"Okay. I understand. You tell them first."

"Thanks for understanding, part of why I love you so much."

Harry's parents were happy the two would marry, but Harry's mother thought it a bit too soon.

"You're just getting going in the business, and Kate is starting a new job. Give it another year, make some money, and become a little more established before you settle into married life."

"I appreciate your advice, Mom, but I'm not worried about our financial situation. I love Kate, and it's time we got married. We'll be fine."

Kate's parents were happy and felt their daughter had a good job and was marrying a man with a bright future. They believed in Harry almost as much as Harry believed in himself. And really liked him, despite his not having a lick of Irish in him. The fact that she loved him, and he loved her, combined with his thoughtfulness in remembering family birthdays or anniversaries, worked for them.

When Harry presented Kate with a small diamond ring a week before the wedding, she was touched. In a white-gold setting, it wasn't the ring they'd talked about her eventually getting, but she made no mention of that. If Harry loved it and thought the silver setting was better than gold, then so did she.

The same was true for their wedding date. Kate had always wanted a spring wedding and imagined the church decorated with spring blooms, her bouquet a simple bunch of daisies. Harry loved the fall, and didn't want to wait until spring, so the fall it was. The church was decorated in fall flowers, and Kate's daisy bouquet went by the wayside. She never even missed it.

The day of their wedding, it was chilly and rainy. Kate remembered asking her mom how she could make it from the limo into the church without getting soaked. Without skipping a beat, her mother had answered, "We'll wrap you in dry-cleaning bags."

Kate smiled at her mother's simple logic. Here she was marrying a dry-cleaning man who was already protecting her. It calmed her fears.

It stopped raining before she left home for the church, and their ceremony went smoothly. Her mother's smile was a clear indication her prayers had been answered.

Harry had planned their five-day honeymoon and, keeping the location a secret, told Kate to pack for warm weather. She assumed they were headed to his parents' Florida condominium, but five days in sunny Jamaica turned out even better. They stayed in a quaint hotel overlooking the ocean and enjoyed strolling around the bustling downtown, bartering in the straw markets, and feasting on conch fritters and chowder. Afternoons were spent lying by the pool sipping frozen daiquiris, capped off by passionate lovemaking at night. All without one word about the dry-cleaning business. Kate was blissfully happy, and Harry seemed just as content.

After returning to earth via the United States, they settled into a small apartment Harry had found just before the wedding. Kate, busy working full time, was happy she didn't have to do the looking. She wasn't thrilled that it faced a noisy main street, but Harry assured her it was set far enough back so noise wouldn't affect them.

Kate trusted Harry's judgment. After three months, she got used to the noise.

Chapter Nine

"What I can't get used to is the roach I found in the butter dish, or the three that scurried under the kitchen cabinet," Kate told Molly when Molly asked how she was adjusting to married life. Kate had moved an hour away from her, but once a month they'd meet halfway for lunch or dinner.

Shuddering, Molly put down her burger. "I've never seen a roach or known anyone who had roaches."

"Me neither. My mother always said roaches meant your house was dirty. The apartment isn't dirty, but the bugs make it feel dirty. Told Harry it's time to move," Kate said as she dug into her French fries.

"Lots of luck with that," Molly said, taking a sip of her soda.

"He's not as tough as you think. He actually called Bob the building manager and demanded the apartment be fumigated. Bob sent out a pest-control company to spray."

"And did he kill the bugs dead?"

"Before they spread? Yes, madam, just like in the bug spray commercial."

What Kate didn't include was the fact that Bob had told her the couple living below them owned a bar.

"Probably bringing them in in liquor boxes. Coming right up the pipes under your sink. Spray will drive them away, but they'll come back," Bob drawled.

"He says they'll be back," Kate reported to Harry later that night when he came home from work. "We need to move. Can't turn on the kitchen light without worrying what will run for cover."

"Got too much going on at work to worry about this. It'll be fine. Let's see if the spray works before we start packing our bags. Don't worry, I'll protect you," Harry said in his most soothing voice as he ran his hand over Kate's hair and gave her a tender kiss. Kate, succumbing to his touch as always, took him at his word, but found herself dreaming of roaches. After she had woken Harry up with her bad roach dreams several nights in a row, Harry finally had enough. He was tired of her nightmares and decided he was even more tired of living with other people's cooking smells and "crap in the hallways." The house hunt began.

After six weeks of looking, they were no closer to leaving the bugs and odors behind. Harry wanted to stay in the suburbs near his parents and his business, and Kate favored living in the city closer to her job at the pharmaceutical company.

Pushing for a downtown condo, Kate pleaded with Harry, "We're too young to be suburbanites. Let's live downtown for a year or two. It'll be fun. We can walk to everything, enjoy more nightlife."

"Come on, Kate, that's not why you want to live downtown. You just want to have a shorter commute. It's not like you're going to be working much longer anyway. Once we have kids, you'll be a full-time mom."

Harry's deciding her future was irritating, but she knew he was right. She'd want to stay home to raise her kids, just like her mom had. Still, she hung on to her argument for a few more beats before giving in.

"I might be able to swing working from home when it gets to that point," she finally reasoned, and put the conversation behind her.

Kate got on the suburban home bandwagon, but she and Harry were still on opposite sides of the fence. She liked an older ranch in a neighborhood with sidewalks, within walking distance of the local downtown. Harry liked a recently remodeled brick bungalow off a busy street.

Not keen on the bungalow's location and concerned there wasn't a garage or a buffer from the road, Kate tried to convince Harry not to buy the house, but he was determined. She put her fears aside after Harry told her he'd build a garage and re-landscape the yard.

"Trust me, the house is perfect," he said. "It's been completely redone, has a first-floor laundry room, and a big basement we could finish off as a TV room. And," he added, "with three bedrooms, it's big enough to start a family and have a guest room for your parents."

The bungalow became their new home. The sprucing up Harry envisioned wouldn't be inexpensive, but Kate was confident that between her income and his, they could handle it.

One new garage and several bushes and trees later,

Kate was satisfied. Harry, pleased his Press Agents business was solvent, went on the hunt for two more locations. After finding two struggling stores not far from his first Press Agents location, he secured a bank loan.

Harry's younger brother, Steve, was on board, excited about helping with the next two stores. He was a great manager and had a knack for finding better ways to do some of the most mundane tasks. But Steve wasn't the only Johnson supporting Harry. Brothers Jack and Jim were cleaning and remodeling the outdated stores.

"My brother Jack's trying to get a house-painting business going and Jim's only working retail, so they can do the remodel," he announced to Kate one morning. "It's a great opportunity for both of them."

"Nice that you can help them out. I'm sure they'll do a good job," Kate said, finishing up her morning coffee.

"They'd better," Harry said as he gulped down the last of his grape pop. Kate never understood how he'd gotten hooked on grape pop, and Harry never understood why it mattered to her. "It's diet, and much better for me than the cream and sugar you put in your coffee," he'd remarked, effectively shutting down any further discussion.

He threw the empty bottle in the trash. "I run a first-class business and won't pay for second-class work."

Kate thought the comment a bit harsh, but simply shook her head, put her cup in the sink, picked up her purse, and gave Harry a kiss goodbye.

Harry's brothers finished remodeling in record time, and despite a few touch-ups Harry demanded, the job had gone smoothly.

"One store's busier than the next, and I'm getting inquiries about commercial cleaning. Time to expand," Harry said to Kate six months later. "Lucky for me an aging storeowner called about buying his under-performing store. Steve and I negotiated a price. We'll be one store stronger."

The Johnson family would soon be one member stronger as well, as Kate was pregnant with their first child. Harry was overjoyed, and before Kate could call her parents, he was on the phone with his mother. She immediately offered to buy the highchair and changing table.

Harry laughed, telling her, "We have a way to go before we need them, but I appreciate the offer."

Kate offered her thanks, and Harry's mother countered with, "You'll have to go to Franzen's in the old neighborhood. It's where I got all my baby furniture. They have solid wood changing tables and highchairs, better than the molded plastic things I see advertised on TV."

Exasperated, Kate said a quick thanks, handed Harry the phone, and went to call her parents on the other line.

"Saints be praised, I'm going to be a granny!" Betty exclaimed. When she relayed the news to Ed, he grabbed the phone, saying, "Katie, my little girl, is going to have a girl!"

"Dad, I've no idea if it's a boy or a girl. We don't want to know ahead of time, so if you have some inside information keep it to yourself," she teased.

"No inside line—just a feeling. Although I wouldn't

mind a wager on it."

After congratulating Harry, Kate's parents were off to tell the aunts, uncles, and neighbors. By the end of the day, more than a few glasses were raised to Katie O'Brien Johnson's baby.

Kate continued to work throughout the pregnancy, despite having to deal with swollen ankles and an enormous belly. Her belly, her mother-in-law reminded her one night after dinner, "might not be so big if you didn't eat so much. Harry says you go out to dinner and come home and start snacking. You'll be sorry. Your extra weight won't just fall off when the baby's born."

Before she could respond in a reasonably nice way, Harry turned to his mother and said, "It's getting late. Have to be at work early tomorrow. Better get going. Thanks for dinner, Mom."

"I enjoyed it," she said, with her typical cringe-worthy smile.

"Wish I could say the same," Kate muttered under her breath. When they got into the car, Harry glanced at a seething Kate.

"You look angry. Don't be so sensitive. Mom's only looking out for your health and the baby's. Plus, you know how disappointed you'll be when your jeans don't fit afterward."

One week early, but not a moment too soon for Kate, eight-pound, ten-ounce Anne came into the world with an ear-piercing wail. She was a chubby, round-faced baby with a cute pug nose, thin lips, and deep blue eyes. Kate thought she was the most beautiful baby she'd ever seen.

Kate's dad declared himself an Irish prophet at having guessed her sex, and her mother declared him half a pint short of a good beer.

Harry's parents, living in the same town, were the new family's first visitors, followed by Father George moments later. George gave Harry a huge hug as Harry's dad gave Kate a large bouquet of pink flowers. Kate was exhausted but happy as she handed Harry's mother her new granddaughter. Cradling the newborn, his mother announced Anne was a "dead ringer for Harry as a baby." Kate took a deep breath at the cliché, just as Harry's dad retrieved Harry's baby pictures from his coat pocket. Kate glanced at the dog-eared photos and smiled. She could see somewhat of a resemblance, but Anne definitely had the O'Brien nose.

Anne was a sweet, easy baby who slept through the night the first month. She was happy even if she missed her long nap, and Kate was happier than she'd ever thought possible. She marveled at Anne's every movement and recorded each little milestone in the baby book Molly had sent her.

"Notice I didn't send you the purse-size album," Molly said when Kate called to thank her for the gift. "You might morph into one of those crazy moms who whips out baby pictures when someone says hello."

"Despite the fact that she's the cutest baby in the world, I'd never do that—at least not at hello," Kate laughed.

As Anne grew to be a toddler, her pleasant disposition grew with her. She rarely made a fuss and could spend hours in her stroller while Kate shopped. She loved watching *Scooby-Doo* cartoons, playing dress-up, and styling her doll's hair. Kate found it all endearing until Anne found her sewing scissors and gave herself a new haircut on her second birthday.

It was time to keep a better eye on Anne, so Kate stopped going into the office, opting to work part-time from home. Harry was happy she cut down her work schedule and always made time to have lunch with them once or twice a week. Any fast-food place was good because the place never mattered, just the time they spent together.

"Don't know if I've ever been happier," Kate said to her mom as she made Anne a peanut-butter-and-jelly sandwich for lunch.

Reaching over to pick up Kate's over-jellied creation, her mom laughed. "A little heavy on the grape jelly, don't you think?"

"Anne would eat it out of the jar with a spoon if I let her. She's as crazy for grape jelly as Harry is for his grape pop."

"Must be genetic," her mom said as she handed Anne the gooey sandwich.

She took a bite with jelly dripping down her chin and onto her white shirt, looking over at Kate. "Thank you, Mommy," she cooed.

Kate kissed Anne on the top of her head and answered, "Mommy loves you, sweet baby." As she mopped the dripping jelly from Anne's shirt, Kate turned to her mom and smiled. "Don't know how life gets better than this."

"Think I've heard you say that before," her mom said with a laugh and an eye roll.

By the time Anne was two and a half, Harry's four locations were on the road to becoming five. Kate worried that buying another store would take Harry away from home more and add financial pressure. To which Harry responded, "Kate, I haven't done too bad so far. You have to trust me. We have a pretty nice lifestyle—never asked you to pinch pennies, all Lincolns aside—because of my expansions. Not one of our friends is doing as well, and I'm sure they wish they had the life we have. I've worked hard. Stop worrying; everything will work out."

Harry, confident in his timing, added a fifth location and brought a general office coordinator named Marcy into the fold. Harry told Kate that Marcy was the perfect choice to keep the business running smoothly. Over time, however, Marcy would contribute her share of wrinkles to their family.

Chapter Ten

Marcy Williams was an insurance company office manager and parishioner of Father George's church. She'd worked the parish fish fry for three years and co-chaired the parish's fundraising auction. A single mother with a seven-year-old son and eight-year-old daughter, she sent her children to the local public school. Father George thought she'd be a perfect fit for Press Agents management and suggested Harry interview her. A higher-paying job would also allow her to send her children to the parish elementary school. Two more school tuitions for Father George.

"Pressure's on," Harry said to George when they met for dinner at a new Japanese restaurant. Harry wasn't keen on Japanese food, but George had convinced him it was time to expand his culinary horizon.

"Have her give me a call." Harry closed the menu and signaled the waiter. "I'll set up an interview. But George, will interviewing her get me a plenary indulgence, or do I have to hire her to qualify?"

"You're taking me back to fifth-grade religion with Sister Lucretia. Last I heard, plenary indulgences went the way of the Latin mass. There may still be some out there, but you, my dear friend, are not a candidate. Focus on ordering. I'm starving."

"Figures. It's always about the greater good with you."

The next day, Marcy came in for an interview. Ten minutes after she'd arrived, Harry knew she was right for the job. Five minutes later, he offered it to her.

"She's personable, smart, asked all the right questions, and comes with five years of management experience. You'll see what I mean when you meet her," he told Kate that night over dinner. "Thanks to George, and some not-so-bad Japanese food, I have a new general manager. I suppose this means I'll have to up my donation to his parish fund."

"Angling to get your name on the new chapel?" Kate teased.

"Maybe not the chapel, but I think I'm classroom worthy."

Rolling her eyes, Kate added, "Hope Marcy is as a good as you've been led to believe. Maybe you'll start coming home at a decent hour."

Marcy proved to be a quick study, and Harry had complete confidence in her. So much so, he decided to take every other Wednesday off to play golf at the club.

"I wasn't sure Harry'd ever let anyone else manage his business, but Marcy has boldly gone where no man has before," Kate said to Molly as she cradled the phone with one hand and wiped off the top of the TV with the other.

"Captain James T. Kirk. *Star Trek*. Loved that show."

"I have to work on getting dinner," Kate said, laughing, as she walked over to turn on the oven. "Talk to you later."

Harry continued to be impressed with Marcy, who came in early, stayed late, and worked one weekend a month. Steve wasn't as impressed.

"You know, Harry, I could have easily done her job, but you passed me over for low-hanging fruit," Steve said as he totaled the day's receipts.

"Come on, Steve, don't be petty," Harry said, looking over his brother's shoulder. "Marcy has much more experience. Things clicked the moment I interviewed her."

"What clicked with you was her bleached blonde hair, tight silk blouses, low-slung pants, and come-and-get-me high heels," Steve mumbled when he closed the books. Harry ignored the comment, reopened the ledger, and was pleasantly surprised at the store's numbers.

Not bad, he thought, *but no sense telling him that, or he'll slack off.*

Three days later when Kate met Marcy, she echoed Steve's comments.

"Dear God, you should see her," she exclaimed to her mom when she'd called.

"I am not God, and you need not use his name in vain," chastised her mom. "Goes against the third command-ment," she added as she made the sign of the cross.

"Sorry. It's just I've never seen a dry-cleaning manager

who looks like a hostess at a strip club. Her makeup is so overdone, and her clothes are so tight and so wrong for the job. And she has this sickeningly sweet way of tilting her head and brushing her hair aside when she talks."

"Don't hold back, tell me what you really think."

Realizing her mother didn't approve of her being so judgmental, Kate defensively tacked on, "And Harry thinks she looks great. He babbles on and on about how well she handles the staff and the customers. I hope she isn't handling Harry."

"Don't be ridiculous. Harry's a good husband and Catholic man. He loves you and Anne. He'd never do anything to hurt you."

Kate knew her mom was right, but Harry's nightly "Marcy this or Marcy that" made her gag. Marcy was a suck-up, and Harry was caught up in perfect-employee euphoria.

When she asked Harry if Marcy ever did anything wrong, he bristled. "What's that supposed to mean? I know she isn't perfect. She's raising two young kids and dealing with a deadbeat ex-husband. Holding a job and paying child support aren't high on his list. I pay her decent money, but she still can't afford a new car or bigger apartment. You are just overreacting."

Harry pulled Kate close and kissed her cheek. "I love you, Kate. Marcy's just a good employee, nothing more."

His words warmed Kate's heart and she added, "Sorry, didn't mean to sound snarky."

But as the weeks went by and Harry's "poor Marcy" litany grew, Kate began to wonder if she wasn't snarky enough. Not sure what to do to stop it, Harry solved the issue when he asked Kate where she shopped for Anne's clothes.

"Why?" Kate asked suspiciously. "Thinking of doing her shopping?"

"Of course not," Harry chided. "Marcy wants to know. She's always going on about how cute Anne is dressed."

"Anne wears basic brands. I'm sure she's seen them."

"Probably not. Said she couldn't afford to shop any-where but a discount store. Even told me she's started shopping secondhand. Can you imagine?"

"No, I can't. But from what I've seen, she isn't getting her clothes anywhere cheap."

"What's that supposed to mean?"

"Nothing," Kate muttered as she walked back to the kitchen. *Get the violins*, she thought. Marcy was playing the "poor me/lucky you" card. Harry was eating it up, and Kate was worried.

Harry's Marcy musings continued until one morning when Kate slammed down his cereal bowl and exploded.

"Will you stop with the Marcy talk? What's going on with you two? The woman doesn't walk on water, and you're not her savior."

Harry quietly responded, "You're paranoid. I love you. Marcy and I have a working relationship. Nothing more. Everything she's done only helps our family."

Kate believed Marcy was close to helping herself to Harry. Either he didn't see it, or he was lying.

Her suspicions grew when she found a blue jewelry box in Harry's car. She'd been looking for some wet ones when she found it in the glove compartment under the owner's manual. When she opened it she saw a thin gold bracelet. Why would Harry have a jewelry box hidden in his glove compartment? With no birthday or anniversary coming up, Kate assumed it wasn't for her.

Filled with dread and despair, she concentrated on giving Anne a bath and getting her into bed before she confronted Harry. A half hour later, Anne was in her pajamas and snuggled in her bed with her favorite blanket. Kate kissed her and added, "Good night, God bless you, sleep tight," as Anne blew her a kiss. Steeling herself for a conversation about Marcy, she headed downstairs to Harry's den.

"What's going on?" she demanded as she walked in and closed the door behind her.

Harry looked up and lowered the volume of the TV. "What do you mean?"

"I was looking for a tissue in your glove compartment and found a jewelry box. Why is it hidden in your car?"

Not missing a beat, Harry answered, "Why are you going through my car? What were you really looking for? The bracelet was a surprise for you, but now you've ruined it. Stop accusing me of being more to Marcy than her boss."

Surprised at Harry's accusations, Kate tried to defend herself. "I'm not accusing you; I'm just asking."

"You need to trust me. Have a bit of self-confidence. I've told you before, Marcy is a great girl and good for business. I love you and wouldn't think of doing anything to hurt you."

Kate wanted to believe him, but a nagging feeling in her stomach continued to indicate something was not right.

Two weeks later, when she met Harry for lunch, she

noticed Marcy had on the same gold bracelet. Kate felt sick to her stomach. Not knowing what to say, she simply commented on how pretty it was. Marcy smiled and said, "Thanks. Glad you like it."

Kate was certain she meant, *Glad you noticed. I know you have one exactly like it.*

Harry said Marcy probably liked Kate's and had bought herself one. Although she didn't want to believe it, Kate was certain Harry had bought Marcy the bracelet. The chance that Harry's "poor little office manager" could shop at a fancy jewelry shop was slim to none.

For weeks after the bracelet incident, Harry said little about Marcy. Kate felt better but still couldn't shake the feeling that Harry was lying to her. When their dinner conversations began to center around Harry peppering her with questions of what she did, where she was going, and what she had planned for the week, Kate's antenna went up.

"Why the sudden interest in where I'm going and what I'm doing?"

"It isn't sudden. I'm always interested," Harry replied in what Kate deemed a syrupy sweet voice. *Dear God*, she said to herself as she looked at him wide-eyed, *he even sounds like her.* He was feeding her a line, but she wasn't sure why. Was he worried he'd run into her when he was with Marcy? Thoughts of them sneaking out and meeting up for an afternoon delight filled her head and hurt her heart. Ready to ask him again if Marcy was more to him than an employee, she stopped short as Harry said, "Wondering how long you're going to keep working. Press

Agents is thriving. You don't need to work. Raising a family is more important than your little part-time job."

Momentarily stunned by his dismissive attitude, Kate took a minute before giving him a one-two punch: "Well, considering you're looking at another new store, and we're having a second baby, I think every little bit helps."

It wasn't quite the way she'd wanted to tell him she was pregnant again, but she was so angry she didn't care.

Harry jumped out of his chair and gave her a big hug and a kiss. "I'm so happy and so blessed you're my wife. Love you so much. Can't wait. When are you due?"

"Too early for an exact date. The doctor says six and a half or seven months from now," Kate said with a wide smile and happy heart.

That night he took her out to the best restaurant in town and ordered her the biggest steak. Kate enjoyed every bite. She hoped things were going to get better, despite Marcy's presence in her life.

Wanting to spend more time with Anne before the new baby came, Kate cut her workdays to Monday and Wednesday. Harry increased his working hours and rarely got home before seven.

When Kate asked him about it, Harry responded, "Want the best for you and my kids. Outside of winning the lotto, this is the way to do it. Relax. Enjoy your last few months of a good night's sleep."

It was hard to argue with Harry's logic; Kate didn't try.

Chapter Eleven

As Harry opened his sixth store and landed his first commercial cleaning contract, Kate delivered a healthy second child and first son.

A pound and a half larger than Anne, Mark's bald head and green eyes were in stark contrast to his blonde, blue-eyed sister.

Not as easy a baby as Anne, Mark had colic and never slept more than an hour or two at a time. Kate was exhausted, but when she asked Harry for help, he shot back with, "Sorry, I can't help out; need my sleep. I'm really busy organizing the new store, and Marcy actually needs more help. She's been working long hours and has childcare issues to boot. Can't afford to lose her. At least you can take a nap during the day."

Like that's going to happen with a toddler and an infant on different schedules, Kate thought. To Harry she said, "Yeah, okay, I get it."

What she also got was that he was not going to give up

a peaceful night's sleep for "the son he always wanted." Harry wasn't much help during the day either. He came home for dinner, ate, read the paper, and retreated to his den for paperwork.

Kate fed both kids, gave them baths, got them ready for bed, and took them in to say goodnight to Harry. It was a routine she loved and hated. She loved bath time with its bubbles, floating toys, and wrinkled fingers. She hated Harry for never giving her a night off. The most he would do is play catch with Anne before bed. Calming her down after a game wasn't easy. Kate could only imagine what it would be like when Mark was Anne's age. She shuddered at the thought, envisioning balls flying around the den taking out anything of value.

Kate's mother called it "roughhousing," a term she said came from Great Britain.

"Ya know, those crazy Brits had rough brawls in their pubs and inns. Not surprising, as they are a small-hearted, chilly bunch that left us starving to death in the potato famine."

A combination of two months' time and changing formulas took Mark from a colicky infant to a seven-hour-a-night sleeper. But just as Mark got settled, Anne began waking up with bad dreams. Kate could easily calm her down, but getting her back to sleep wasn't as easy.

After two nights of being unable to fall back to sleep after soothing Anne, Kate brought the frightened child into bed with her and Harry. By the fifth night, Harry was complaining. The sixth night, Kate started sleeping in Anne's bed.

Sleeping with a four-and-a-half-year-old in a twin bed left Kate with an aching back and stiff neck. Alone in their queen-size bed, Harry slept like a hibernating bear. Kate was tired and cranky and decided it was time to ask Harry for help.

"Maybe you should stop giving her juice before bed; the sugar probably winds her up," he suggested as he looked over the evening newspaper. "Watching that *Home Alone* movie doesn't help either. She's probably scared that creepy guys are going to break into our house too."

"So, ditch the juice and the movie and presto, problem solved. Why didn't I think of that?"

"Come on, Kate, you asked; I gave you my opinion." He tossed the paper aside. "That's all I got. Check that Dr. Spock book my mom gave you."

"That book was published in the late '40s. Think things have changed a bit since then."

Harry shook his head. "My mother swears by Spock. He's the best. If you think you know better than a professional, try it your way. Either way, Anne needs to stop this. You need sleep. You're not thinking straight."

You're right, she thought. *If I were thinking straight, I never would have asked you in the first place.*

Despite Anne's continuing her juice habit before bed and despite watching her favorite movie, she eventually conquered her fears and began sleeping all night. It was a small victory for Kate then—though years later, she realized the current experts were giving parents the same advice Harry had given her. She could have mentioned it to him, but she didn't.

A Pressing Affair

Mark grew to be a happy toddler but was stronger-willed than Anne. Unless the stroller was constantly moving, he screamed to get out. Kate tried distracting him with Anne's favorite juice and pretzels, but he'd send them flying back at her. "No" was his first word and Houdini should have been his middle name. There wasn't a crib, car seat, or highchair from which he couldn't escape.

"Yesterday I let him out of the grocery cart hoping he'd quiet down. I turned around, and he took off," Kate relayed to her sister over lunch. "I ran down the aisle after him and right into old Mrs. Peterson and her two jars of pickles. She panicked and backed into the stock boy loading hot dog and hamburger buns on the shelf. He let out a, 'What the fuck?' She screamed, and the pickles were airborne."

"Talk about being in a pickle!"

"Not funny. The pickles landed in the buns, and Mrs. Peterson whacked the stock boy with her purse. All of which gave Mark time to climb into the dairy case to get to the hot dogs."

Choking on her iced tea, her sister coughed out, "Was the mission successful?"

"No. I pulled him out of the cooler and said, 'Come on, little boy, let me help you find your mother.' I know someday I'll be laughing about this, but it was a bit unnerving," Kate said with a small chuckle.

"Might make for a great story someday at his rehearsal dinner," Sue added.

"Hmm, he's never going to get married; no woman will be good enough for my boy!" Kate said, raising her glass to take a long drink of wine.

Life with a six-year-old and a two-and-a-half-year-old was hectic, but Kate didn't want anyone else doing her job. Her professional career was over, and her days were filled with household chores, playtime at the park, story time at the library, and swimming lessons.

As Kate became CEO of the family, Harry continued his quest to make Press Agents the only place to go for dry cleaning. In two short months, he bought two additional stores and now had eight. With expansion came longer working hours, later family dinners, and an exhausted Harry out cold on the couch most nights.

He joined his parents' country club, bought season tickets to pro basketball and baseball, and collected rare French wines for an eventual wine cellar.

"My businesses are doing exceptionally well. It's time to enjoy more of the fruits of my labors," he announced to Kate.

"We've already taken two cruises, bought new cars, had the yard re-landscaped and the deck rebuilt," Kate said, exasperated.

"We need a bigger house and a better yard for the kids. I'd like to build a pool. Have enough space for one of those big wooden play sets. There's a vacant lot near the center of town. Think we should look at it."

The next day, they looked at the heavily treed four-acre property, decided they loved it, and offered the seller full price. After six months of meeting with architects and builders, Harry approved the plans and hired Marcy's brother-in-law as general contractor.

"Know you think it's been a long, drawn-out process, but I want the house to be perfect," he said to Kate. "It's your job to get a professional decorator on board. This project's too big for you to handle."

Kate bristled at Harry's comment but figured he was probably right. She chose a local decorator and Harry commented, "Hope she's up to the job. Not all that impressed with her or her ideas."

"I like her. It'll work out just fine. She's not going to sell me on anything I don't want," Kate said.

"Not so sure about that," Harry mumbled.

A year later, the house that Kate termed "the house Harry built" was finished. At twelve thousand square feet, the stone-and-stucco house was the talk of the town. As it was being built, Kate had overheard two women talking about the "new hotel" being built. "Took me a minute to realize they were talking about our house," Kate told Molly. "It's Harry's monument to Harry, and he'll never leave it," she'd added. "We'll have to bury him in the backyard between his basketball court and that ridiculous walking path."

"Nah," Molly said, shaking her head. "I think you'll have to dig a hole in the front yard under the flagpole in his damn stone reflection garden. Think he'll want an eternal flame?"

Chapter Twelve

Although not as infamous as Walt Disney's thirty-thousand-garment-a-day dry-cleaning facility, Press Agents was no Mickey Mouse operation. With sixty employees and eight locations, it was the largest dry-cleaning company in Michigan. Harry was Press Agents proud.

"I'm looking at adding two larger stores for cleaning non-clothing items like boots and rugs," he told Kate as they watched Anne's baseball game. "It was Marcy's idea. She's also suggested ads touting, 'The Press Agents family handles all your family's cleaning needs—except your teeth.'"

"That's a catchy slogan," Kate drolly replied as she stood to cheer for Anne. It was the last inning, and Anne was at bat. She swung at the first two pitches and missed. The next two were balls. One pitch later, she struck out. Her team lost three to two.

"She's not keeping her eye on the ball. She's swinging

too soon," Harry disgustedly said to Kate. "I've told her that thousands of times. She's not concentrating."

"Ease up. She's almost a teenager. There's more to life than baseball. Giver her a break—she had two hits in practice yesterday."

"I don't care about practice. It's the game that counts. Going to have to work with her more. I hope she's not afraid of the ball like her mother!"

Caught between anger and hurt, and not sure why Harry's little criticisms still surprised her, Kate reeled in her emotions.

"I'm going to get Anne," she said as she stood up to leave. "See you and Mark at home."

When she pulled into the driveway, Harry was playing catch with Mark in the front yard.

"Hey, Anne, get your mitt. You need to practice," Harry yelled. "And grab a bat from the garage."

Looking at Kate with "help me" eyes, Anne turned and slowly walked to the garage.

"It'll be okay, Anne. Your dad's just trying to help you get better. Shaking her head, Kate strode over to Harry. "How about you take a break for lunch. I'll make mac and cheese, and I have fresh glazed donuts for dessert. Anne could use a little lunch."

"What Anne could use is more practice. Take Mark in and give him something to eat. Anne will be in when we're done."

Kate started to ask him to take it easy on Anne—then thought better of it. Harry would do what he wanted, and she would end up smoothing things over when Anne got upset. It was how things worked. Kate was confident it wouldn't change anytime soon.

Harry followed through on his expansion plans and bought two larger stores. Marcy was promoted to personnel and acquisitions manager. Her friend Bonnie was hired to manage Marcy's stores. When Kate met Bonnie, she almost laughed out loud.

"Bonnie is a Marcy look-alike and just as annoying," she told her sister. "They're both perky little things who wear too much makeup and too little clothes. They look like bad cocktail waitresses in a cheap bar. Still can't believe Harry hired them."

Sue laughed. "Maybe he was thinking ahead. Getting the girls in place for the ultimate Press Agents experience: martinis and martini-izing. Better yet, Marcy and martini-izing at Press Agents!"

"Don't let Harry hear that. He might just do it. Drinks at the dry cleaners. Nothing good coming from that!"

As Kate worried about the Marcy/Bonnie contingent, Harry worried about Steve.

"Steve is taking over the two new stores, but I'm not sure he's up to it. I only gave them to him to stop him from moaning about being passed over. Like when we were kids, and I didn't pick him for our team. Why would I? He wasn't much of an athlete. Never practiced," Harry said to Kate as they watched Mark's basketball game.

"Maybe sports aren't for everyone."

"Says someone who's never played a game in her life."

"Not true. I played a lot of miniature golf as a kid. I was the Timber Trails champion. I walked away with a trophy and a month of free golf."

"We called it putt-putt. I was the Johnson putt-putt king. My brothers couldn't beat me there either. Still can't."

About to comment on his one-upmanship, Kate spied Mark standing at the free-throw line. Both his shots went in. Harry cheered and turned to Kate. "See that, Kate? That's what practice does. Mark listens. He gets it."

"Don't let Anne hear you say that," Kate scolded. "It'll only hurt her feelings."

"I know what Anne needs, and it's not you babying her," Harry said.

Kate's maternal instinct kicked in. "Don't be such a hard-hearted Hannah."

"What's that supposed to mean? Another one your crazy lyrics games?" Harry spat back as he put on his coat.

The basketball game was over and so was their conversation. Kate picked up her purse and silently followed Harry down the steps to get Mark.

Thankful Mark spent the ride home going on and on about the game and the bad calls, Kate stared out the car window. She sensed something wasn't right with Harry. His temper was shorter and he seemed to delight in hurting her. She had, at first, attributed it to the pressures of his growing business, but when their bedroom became a place only for sleeping, she was concerned. Harry had never been much of a romantic, but as the days became weeks without any sex or intimacy, Kate went on the offense. Maybe she'd become too much of a mom. Her flannel nightgowns, socks, and foot cream had to go. It was time to up her game.

One shopping trip and a few hundred dollars later, she was ready.

"It felt kind of weird being in a store we used to laugh about in college," she said to Molly.

"That was then. We're not so young and firm anymore. We—and I mean me too—need satin, silk, and lace to get the job done."

"But 'You Can't Hurry Love.'"

"I'm not playing when the game's that easy. Any self-respecting Supremes fan would demand you 'Stop! In the Name of Love.'" She laughed, but there was sadness and longing under the laughter. The game just wasn't as much fun as it used to be.

When Kate's lacy underwear and silk pajamas went unnoticed, she decided that wearing no clothes might do it. She stripped down to her bare bones; Harry grinned and got into bed.

Her face dropped. "Am I doing something wrong? You barely notice me. I know you don't like to talk about our sex life, but—."

Harry quickly cut her off. "No, that's not it. You know I love you. I'm just so stressed out at work. I wasn't going to say anything, but I just got these new vitamins I saw advertised in *USA Today*. They're supposed to help with...well, you know."

"With what?"

"Performance."

Tempted to shoot back with, "What performance? Can't remember your lines?" Kate bit her tongue. She was hurt and confused. There must be something wrong with her. Why else would Harry be having issues.

"You know," he said, looking her in the eyes, "it took a lot of courage for me to order these pills. I hope you appreciate it."

Let's hope they work she thought as she leaned over and gave him a long, deep kiss. That too failed to get a reaction; and Harry turned over and went to sleep. The only performance that night was Harry's snoring.

The next morning, Harry's good dad performance was outstanding. He poured cereal for the kids, got them juice, and packed their lunches and put them into their book bags. Kate thanked Harry for his help and gave the kids a quick kiss goodbye. Anne smiled and said, "Love you too, Mom," as Mark wiped her mom kiss off. Kate smiled as she realized her eleven-year-old son was growing up.

"Oh, and Mom," Mark said as he turned to go, "I have practice; pick me up at four."

"You don't need to remind me—it's on my calendar."

"Try to be on time," Harry interjected. "You're always running late. Last time Mark thought you weren't coming."

"Last time I was late because I took your mom to the doctor and he was running late."

"Ah, now it's my mom's fault," Harry said as he followed the kids out the door.

"Give it a rest," Kate mumbled as she walked back to clean up the breakfast dishes. Harry was getting more and more impatient with her, and she couldn't understand what she was doing to irritate him. Probably work, she reasoned as she headed out to the grocery store. Seemed like she spent half her life buying food, cooking meals, and packing lunches. Seemed like a lifetime ago when she only had to worry about herself. But that's what she signed on for and, in reality, she wouldn't have changed a thing.

That afternoon, Harry sent her an enormous bunch of daisies in a crystal vase. Stunned at his sudden kindness, Kate called to thank him. He seemed more like his old self, laughing and joking. The conversation ended with Harry saying he knew things were going to get better. Not sure if it was the new vitamins talking, she took him at his word. His word wasn't as easy to take when the morning mail arrived.

Chapter Thirteen

A DMV envelope containing what Kate assumed was her driver's license renewal had arrived. Tearing open the envelope also tore open her heart. Inside was a grainy red-light camera photo of Harry and Marcy. Kate's hands began to shake. She couldn't catch her breath. Was this really happening? Harry and Marcy were a couple? Looking at the citation more closely, she noticed the time stamp of 7:02, the Saturday she was at her sister's lake house with the kids. Too exhausted to make the two-hour drive, Harry had opted out.

She recalled he'd said he was going to catch up on paperwork and watch football. He hadn't called her that night but did so early the next morning. He'd never said anything about meeting Marcy.

The ticket drifted out of her hand, and as she bent to pick it up, she did a double take. Marcy was driving Harry's car. Harry was next to her.

Kate wasn't even allowed to drive his prized sports car.

Where were they going? Why hadn't Harry said anything?

Trying to sort it all out, she was distracted when Anne ran in whining, "When are we leaving? I want to see them feed the lions! Why's it taking so long?"

"I'm going as fast as I can," she snapped.

"Sor-ree," Anne drawled.

"No, sorry I snapped at you. I'll grab the lunch basket from the fridge and be right out. Go ahead and get in the car. Buckle up."

She wanted to call Harry but was afraid of what he'd say. Unsure of what to do next, she did what came naturally: staying busy by taking the kids to the zoo.

When Harry came home that night, Kate was waiting at the open door. As soon as she saw him pull in the garage, she started crying. A confused Harry looked over at Kate.

"What's wrong? Are Mark and Anne all right?"

"They're fine," she said, swiping at her teary cheeks. "I'm angry. I trusted you."

"What are you talking about?"

"I'm talking about this," she said as she pushed the ticket into his chest. "Why was Marcy driving your car? Why did you lie to me?"

The ticket fluttered to the ground, and stooping over to pick it up, he looked at it and laughed.

"It's not what you think. After we pitched the hotel contract, I let her drive back to the office. She's never driven anything better than her low-end sedan, so I thought she'd get a kick out of driving my car. Nothing's going on. This is all in your head."

Putting his arms around her, he added, "I honestly forgot to tell you. There's nothing to worry about. I love you, Kate." He steered her toward the kitchen. "Now, come on, forget about it. Let's eat dinner."

His explanation was plausible, but she knew he was lying. That night when everyone was in bed, she snuck downstairs looking for evidence. Going through Harry's coat pockets, desk drawers, and his wallet yielded a gas receipt, two pieces of gum, and a mint from their club. Next up was his phone. She checked recent calls. He'd been calling Marcy right after he'd call Kate. Coincidence? Unlikely.

She headed back to bed with nothing but a pounding headache to show for her sleuthing.

The next morning, Harry reminded her he had an appointment at the acupuncturist. His back had been giving him trouble, and when his internist failed to get him pain-free, he turned to alternative medicine. George swore the doctor could work miracles, and that was good enough for Harry.

"I'll be home late 'cause my appointment is at four. The doctor is always running behind, and traffic will be miserable. No idea what time I'll be done. Go ahead and eat without me. Oh," he added as he turned to leave, "you're welcome to call and confirm my appointment. I'll have the office send you the number."

"I don't need to do that. Sad you think I'd check up on you."

"Sad or not, I'll get you the number," Harry added as he slammed the door behind him.

Kate felt miserable. Maybe it was all in her head. She remembered how Harry's father's affair had devastated his family, and she couldn't imagine Harry doing the same thing. Harry loved her, and she him. She just needed to try harder. So, try she did when she called him and asked to meet for lunch. She figured bringing Anne and Mark would be a good diversion. Anne wore her favorite pink pants and striped top. She had wanted to wear mascara and lip gloss, but Kate nixed it. "You dad's not so keen on make-up. Stick with your natural beauty."

Anne let out a large sigh. "Dad still thinks I'm a little girl. I'm almost an adult."

Kate laughed. *Better not tell him that*, she thought. Smiling to herself, she went to check on Mark. He was already outfitted in his best Harry look-alike garb: khaki pants, a button-down plaid shirt, and top siders.

As she drove to Harry's, she looked in the rearview mirror at the kids. Anne was scrolling through her phone and Mark was playing a game on his iPad. She loved them more than she ever thought possible. She couldn't imagine Harry throwing this all away.

When they pulled into the Press Agents lot, Kate's heart fell when she spotted Marcy's car. It wasn't unusual, but it wasn't what she wanted to face that day. She wanted to turn the car around and head home. But she resisted the urge to put it in reverse and parked. She quickly refreshed her lipstick, ran a comb through her hair, and got out of the car. Mark and Anne were already out of the car and moving through the parking lot.

"Slow down, watch out for cars coming in the parking lot," she cautioned as she hurried to catch up.

"We're fine, Mom. Geez, we're not babies," Anne said, exasperated.

"Yeah, Mom, you're just too slow," Mark shot back.

Before she could say any more, Harry had come out the door to meet them. Happy to see the kids, he gave Anne a hug and tousled Mark's hair. He asked Kate for a minute to talk to Bonnie as they followed him into the building.

As they waited, Kate glanced around Harry's office at Anne's and Mark's drawings, school pictures, and an assortment of "Great Dad" Father's Day gifts. On his desk, the gold first-anniversary clock Kate had given him sat to the right of the leather desk pad commemorating their seventh anniversary. A picture of Harry's parents was on the credenza flanked by photos taken on their last two cruises. *Harry is all about family,* she thought as she drank it all in. She was proud of him and loved him with all her heart.

When Harry returned, Marcy followed.

"Don't mean to hold you up, just wanted to say hello and see the kids. I can't believe how grown up they are," Marcy gushed.

Looking at Marcy, Harry added, "Yeah, before we know it, they'll both be in college and out the door. I'm getting so old."

Marcy looked back at Harry. They briefly made eye contact. Kate saw something pass between them and felt a lump in her throat but silently warned herself not to show the emotions roiling in her stomach.

Their lunch went smoothly, as both Anne and Mark had a lot to say. *Thank the Lord,* Kate thought as she struggled to eat her salad, finding it almost impossible to swallow. When Harry announced it was time for him to get back to work, she quickly threw her half-eaten lunch away. Her iced tea followed. Harry didn't notice and the kids were focused on their food.

They drove Harry back to his office, and he kissed the kids goodbye. Kate got a shoulder squeeze and a promise of dinner at their favorite Italian restaurant.

Chapter Fourteen

How involved and for how long were the questions tugging at Kate's heart. If she told Harry she thought he and Marcy were having an affair, would he fall back on the "It's all in your head" excuse? Worse yet, what would she do if he admitted it? He'd have to move out. Then what? She had two children and a husband who controlled their purse strings. Would he support them, or would she have to fight for every dollar?

Making herself frantic with worry wasn't going to help. She needed advice.

"You might think I'm crazy," she said when she called Sue, "but I think Harry's carrying on with Marcy. First it was the ticket incident, and today when I met him for lunch, I saw something pass between them. It was just a look, but there was something more there. I could feel it. I love him so much—don't know what to do."

"You might be reading too much into all of this. Can't see Harry cheating with the likes of Marcy. She may be smitten with him and his big fat wallet, but don't think Harry would cross the line. He's probably just flattered she's giving him the eye. He may be treading on dangerous ground, but he knows how good he has it with you and the kids."

"Not so sure. If he isn't lamenting how hard Marcy's life is, he's boasting about how important she is to his business. I feel like Marcy is taking over. I'm afraid she's stealing my husband. I don't know how to stop it."

There was a long pause on the other end of the line. Kate could almost hear Sue's mind turning.

"Can you talk to Harry, tell him you're worried?"

"No. He'll say I'm crazy. Won't listen to me. When I asked him how wise it was to put so much stock in a high school graduate, he hit me with, 'She wasn't as lucky as you or me. You're a bit snooty, aren't you? Your own mother never went to college.' Then he tacked on, 'Your life isn't so bad for someone from a very ordinary Irish neighborhood.' I wanted to slap him."

"That was hitting below the belt."

"Yeah, I know. I hit back with, 'It's not like I was the poor little match girl you rescued from the cold,'" Kate said, remembering how empowered she'd felt saying it.

"Ah, not living happily ever after?"

"Yeah, our fairy-tale life is looking more like a nightmare." Kate's momentary feelings of power were shattered by the unavoidable distinction between fairy tales and reality. And drifting through her mind was a question she couldn't quite answer: why did she love him so much and believe in him more than herself?

That night on their way to dinner Harry was unusually quiet. Kate hardly noticed. She was too busy nervously rattling on about Anne's new teacher and Mark's new basketball coach. Exhausting those two subjects, she moved on to her parents' new puppy.

"That crazy dog does a lot of damage. It dug up my mom's pansies and gnawed off the corner of the coffee table. Yesterday, he snatched a package of hot dogs off the counter. Ate the whole pack! Not the packaging. Guess he has standards."

"Don't get why your parents bought a dog. Such a dumb idea. They both work," Harry said as they pulled into the restaurant lot.

"Well, my mom—" Kate began.

Harry interrupted, "Go in and get us a table. I'll park the car. Oh, and Kate," he added as she got out, "don't let them put us near the kitchen again."

She nodded, thought about clicking her heels together and saluting, but held back. Harry's delivery was curt, but she didn't disagree. She had no desire to catch a glimpse of what might be a not-so-clean kitchen. Kate remembered Molly, who'd waitressed in college, saying, "It's better to enjoy the food without seeing where it comes from."

With faded Italian murals, red-checkered plastic tablecloths, and straw-bottled candles, the restaurant bordered on campy. It was a Johnson family favorite. Harry's parents were on a first-name basis with Angelo, the owner. Angelo had always stopped by their table to say hello. He did the same for Harry. Kate suspected it was the reason they often ate there.

By the time they were seated and had ordered, the restaurant had filled up. She was nervous and felt ill at ease. Would Harry bring up Marcy? Could she hold herself back from getting into an argument with him?

Looking back, Kate was thankful for the bustling crowd. "No one paid any attention to what was going on with Harry and me. Spared me embarrassment. Spared Harry's life," she told her sister afterward.

Kate kept the conversation light and avoided bringing up anything to do with Press Agents. Harry listened and sipped his wine. As the minutes ticked by and Kate anxiously searched for funny stories about the kids, Harry said nothing.

As she reached for some bread, a vision of Harry's mom came into her head. "Can't believe your mom puts up with this mushy Italian wannabe bread," she joked.

Harry looked at her and said nothing.

Frustrated and wanting to elicit some sort of response, she tacked on, "Not saying your mom's wrong. I was..."

Harry held up his hand, stopping Kate midsentence. Thinking she'd crossed a family line, she waited for his angry response. She was shocked to see a sheepish smile light up his face.

"Kate, I want you to know I have deep feelings for Marcy."

"What?" she cried out in horror as she began to shake. "You have what?"

Must not have heard him right, Kate thought as she dropped her bread. Looking down at her plate and then up at Harry, she knew she had. He was smiling at her. Was this some sort of joke?

Harry let out a slow breath as if someone had lifted the weight off his shoulders. Kate felt like a giant weight had settled on her chest. It was so painful, she thought she might be having a heart attack.

Her dad said his heart attack was like having an elephant sit on his chest. *That must be what's happening to me*, she thought as she struggled with the pain. Not sure what to do or say, she pushed back from the table. She had to make it all go away. She sprang to her feet, knocked over her chair, and ran to the bathroom.

She bolted the door behind her and slid down to the floor. Her tears became slow sobs as her mind raced. What about their marriage? Was he leaving her? What should she do?

What she thought she'd do was throw up, but her retching produced only dry heaves. She pulled at her hair, slammed her fist into the paper towel container, and cursed God and all the saints.

Her internal rant didn't make her feel better, but when she heard a knock on the door, she knew she'd have to pull herself together. She got up, rinsed her face, smoothed her hair, and opened the door to the woman who was waiting.

"Sorry," she whispered, still choking back tears. Hoping Harry would tell her it was nothing, that his feelings for Marcy would pass, she straightened her skirt and marched back to the table, though her show of confidence was more an act than a reality.

Harry looked up from his wine as if he hadn't a care in the world. Kate stared at him in disbelief. In a flash of Irish temper, she raised her hand to slap him.

Sensing what was coming, he took her arm.

"Calm down," he said quietly as he pulled out her chair. "Sit down. You know I love you. It's not like I want to leave you and the kids. I just have these feelings. I want to be with her. Take her out to the movies, nice dinners, and—"

"And what, Harry?" Kate asked with false bravado. "Stay married to me and date your low-life employee?"

"That was uncalled for."

"You have no idea what this calls for. Consider yourself lucky I'm not throwing my pasta at you," she snarled.

"You need to control yourself," Harry calmly responded.

"You need to get the check. You're a son of a bitch and a pompous asshole. I hate you," she hissed, and she stormed out of the restaurant.

They rode home in silence. As they pulled into the garage, Kate's tears returned, spilling down her face onto her sweater. Wiping at her eyes with the back of her hand, she turned to Harry.

"What the hell is wrong with you? Why would you do this to us? You're throwing everything away for a hop in the hay?"

"Typical Kate. Never listens. Never said I was throwing anything away."

That did it. Kate followed through with a slap. As a volley of crude words spilled out, she cautioned him, "Cover your ears, you little prick." She got out of the car, then turned, leaned back in, and hurled her Marcy look-alike bracelet at Harry.

Chapter Fifteen

That night she slept in the guest bedroom. Lying in the dark with hot tears spilling down her face, she wondered if things would be better in the morning. Needing to curtail her gut instincts and ally her fears, she did some deep breathing followed by her nightly prayers. She felt a bit better and reasoned Harry would come to his senses. It was comfort enough to get her a few hours of sleep.

The next morning, Harry did what he always did on Saturdays. He played golf.

Kate, desperately needing support and feeling as if she were about to crack into tiny pieces that no amount of glue could fix, spent most of the day on the phone with her sister and mother. Both were floored by Harry's "feelings" for Marcy. When her mom suggested marriage counseling, Kate replied, "Harry Johnson get counseling? Don't you know him?"

"I know he's been a good man and father. No doubt this little hussy's turned his head, but you don't know what, if anything, happened. You need a marriage counselor. Maybe Father George can suggest someone."

Her sister suggested something not as ecumenically sound. "That conniving little bitch has to go. If Harry hasn't crossed the line, she'll make sure he does. He's a pretty nice meal ticket for her and her creepy kids. He has to fire her."

Kate agreed. Though Harry hadn't said he'd strayed, she was sure he had. Guilt had made him confess his feelings for Marcy. What the hell were these "feelings"? Harry-speak for love and sex? The thought of Harry hooking up with Marcy made her sick.

How do other women cope with this? Kate wondered. *Do they want details? Do they hire a detective? Do they visualize their husbands with the other woman? Or do they block it all out, hoping it will just go away?* It was too much to process. Not knowing what to do next was solved when Mark came bounding down the stairs.

"Got to be at practice in ten minutes. Let's go!"

Kate did what she'd always done—she kept going. She grabbed her purse, left a note for the cleaning lady, and flew out the door. After she dropped Mark off, she stopped at the grocery store. Big mistake. Kate knew empty-stomach shopping led to overbuying, but she wasn't prepared for broken-heart shopping. Chips or pretzels? Cheese and crackers or guac and chips? Unable to choose, she chose them all. Shortbread cookies and bite-size muffins followed. She almost went for ice cream but thought better of it. *I refuse to be some bad movie stereotype drowning in vats of ice cream*, she thought.

Buoyed by a sudden bout of self-confidence, she added two bottles of wine to her cart.

Looking down at her selections, she smiled. Anne and Mark would be thrilled. Junk food heaven. Hoping to restore some healthy-eating sanity, she tossed in a head of lettuce, carrots, celery, and apples.

After picking Mark up from basketball and stopping at the drive-thru, she felt better. Was it because of Mark's play-by-play account of practice or her Big Mac and fries? Didn't matter. She was energized. Ready to fight this head on. Marcy goes or Harry goes. She'd force him to decide. Time for him to rein in his adolescent feelings and revert to the good, honest man she'd married.

When Harry returned from golf, and the kids were out of earshot, Kate presented her ultimatum. He clenched his teeth and glared at her. Said nothing. Buoyed by her anger, Kate spat out, "If you won't fire her, you have to move out. It's her or me. You decide." Harry was furious. It had never occurred to him that Kate wouldn't understand what Marcy meant to him. He didn't want to fire her and didn't want to leave. He listened and said nothing. Picking up his coat, he turned to Kate and said, "Going to talk to George."

"Thinking of moving in with him at the rectory?"

Harry shook his head. "Always have to be sarcastic, don't you?"

In an attempt to right the ship, Harry met George at the rectory and asked him for advice.

"Marcy's the driving force behind my business. I like

going to work because she's there," he said as he sat down in one of George's comfortable leather chairs. George's office had rich wood paneling, deep pile carpeting, a mahogany desk, and buttery-soft dark-leather chairs. The room faced a large garden and enjoyed the bright light of the morning sun and cool afternoon breezes from three tall, leaded-glass windows. It was George's private oasis and far different than the rest of the outdated and rundown rectory. Harry took a minute to drink in the peacefulness before he sat forward, exclaiming, "She has my back. She thinks like I do. I need her there. Kate won't budge. I need time, and Kate isn't willing to give me any."

"Knowing Kate, what did you expect?" George asked as he walked over to an antique cabinet to pour them each a brandy. "She's tough. Having crossed her over songs for Mark's christening mass, I've seen her stubborn and demanding side."

"Yeah," Harry agreed as he reached for his glass. "But how do I decide what's best for me? Besides a dinner or two, I haven't been able to take Marcy out—spend time with her and get to know her on a more personal level. I've only met her kids once or twice."

George hesitated and swirled his brandy, before making the shift from priest to confidant.

"If you need to test the waters, go away with her for a weekend. One of my Jesuit friends has a Bahamas condo. I'm sure you could use it. Kate doesn't need to know. It'll help you make a decision. Trust me. I'm looking out for you just like I did in high school."

"Yeah, yeah, I remember. It's not something a guy ever forgets. Don't need to bring up the past. I'm trying to figure out my future. I have a family, a successful business.

People look up to me."

"Take my advice. Head to the Bahamas," George said, and he finished his drink.

Taking George's advice was something Harry always felt comfortable doing. George always knew what was best for Harry and on more than one occasion had saved him from himself. He left the rectory feeling better than he had in days, though he was surprised George hadn't tacked on a trip to the confessional. He must have decided Harry's relationship with Marcy was only an affair of the heart. If George had bought it, he could convince Kate of the same.

Mulling over their conversation, he got into his car just as his phone rang. He was surprised to hear Kate's angry voice.

"Where are you, Harry? I've been calling you all afternoon. Too busy with your babe to take phone calls?"

Harry cut her off. "Knock it off, Kate. I was with George. What's up?"

"Sorry, it's Mark. He's developed this rash. His fever of just over a hundred this morning is up to 102.5. I've called the doctor, but I'm scared. He's really lethargic and—"

"I'm on my way. I remember my mom saying a tepid bath helps. Start the water. Stay calm. I'll be home before you know it. He will be fine."

Kate kept reasonably calm till Harry got home.

"I'm sorry," she said, teary-eyed, when he rushed into the house. "There is so much going wrong with us. What'll I do if Mark ends up in the hospital?"

"He's not going to end up in the hospital. The bath and another dose of aspirin will break the fever. Everything's going to be okay. Trust me."

In retrospect, Harry's asking Kate to trust him should have put her on high alert. Used car dealers and personal injury lawyers were always touting their trustworthiness and it always made her laugh. But this was Harry, and she loved him and trusted him to do the best for them. Mark's fever broke and he perked up with juice and a cherry popsicle.

Kate was grateful Harry had come through, but she felt wrung out. Tempted to break open a bottle of wine, she resisted the urge, opting for candy and chips instead.

With Mark's fever down and Kate calm, Harry retreated to his den to check in with Marcy. Anxious to tell her of his Bahamas plans, he was stopped short.

"Why haven't you called?" Marcy snapped when she heard his voice. "The office said you left in a hurry. What's going on? Problem with your whiny wife and kids?"

Harry was momentarily at a loss for words.

"My son is sick. Really don't want to listen to this."

"And I don't want to be sitting around waiting for you. You said we'd have lunch today. Never heard from you. You didn't even bother to let me know what's going on. I deserve better than this."

Harry gritted his teeth so hard he could barely release his jaw. He slammed his fist on his desk. His letter opener and a stack of papers flew to the floor. He pushed it all aside with his foot as he stood up. Walking around his desk, he closed the door, and with a deep breath quietly said, "Sorry to upset you." He paused and added, "This isn't working out."

"Of course it is," Marcy said, more annoyed than upset. She could handle Harry. "You're just being dramatic. Get a grip!"

"I have a grip." Harry interrupted her before she could go on. He wanted to follow with, "You just talked yourself out of a trip to the Bahamas," but he wasn't sure it was really off the table. Maybe this outburst was an aberration. Maybe she'd apologize for her intolerable behavior and things between them would revert to normal.

His thoughts of a sun-and-sex-soaked holiday were dashed, however, when Marcy asked, "How do you think you'd manage Press Agents without me? You're going to ruin everything we built."

"I built Press Agents. You simply helped," Harry corrected her. Then he slammed down the phone.

That was all it had taken to put him over the "who stays/who goes" edge. No one had built his business for him. He'd done it all on his own, thanks to his dedication and determination. Marcy sounded as un-understanding and demanding as Kate. No sense in trading one for the other. He loved his kids and wasn't sure he could feel the same about Marcy's kids.

Marcy wasn't the mother Kate was, nor would she ever be. Her *comme ci comme ça* attitude would eventually make him crazy. And how would his kids react if he suddenly moved out? How would they feel about expanding their family by adding two children? No, if he abandoned them, Kate would make sure they would never forgive him. She'd do to him what his mother had done to his dad: turn the kids against him. He'd rather spend a few months inconvenienced, finding Marcy's replacement.

Anxious to put the whole issue behind him, the next day Harry told Kate that Marcy was leaving. He never said he was sorry and appeared more angry than contrite, but Kate took it for what it was. He'd done as she had asked.

That night in bed Harry's stellar performance made Kate realize just how much she'd missed having sex for so many months. She was happy and relieved. He really did love her. The old Harry was back. Their home and love life would return to normal.

Chapter Sixteen

Two weeks later, Marcy was little more than a bad memory for Harry. Kate tried to convince herself that she had won, that Harry was sorry he had hurt her, but snippets of the past kept tripping her up. Flashes of Marcy seeped through the cracks in their relationship, though she somehow always managed to pave over them.

"I don't want to talk about this again," Harry announced one night as they got into bed. "I did what you asked. You need to get past this, Kate." He reached over to turn off the light. "I've got to focus on restructuring my business. Don't have time to be distracted."

The great Oz has spoken, Kate mused as she got under the covers. Funny thing, he'd had time to be distracted by Marcy. What had put a lid on his feelings was a mystery to her, but Kate didn't allow herself to spend time guessing or even thinking about it. She was thankful Marcy was gone. Maybe Harry was right. Maybe it was time to put it behind them.

"I think things between us will finally get back to normal," she told her mom the next morning. "I'm going to counseling. Harry won't. Says he doesn't want a stranger telling him how to run his life."

"Maybe he's embarrassed. There's nothing wrong with getting help. If you had a broken leg, you wouldn't expect it to heal itself. You'd see a doctor. Same goes for a broken marriage."

"I know that, but that doesn't change things for Harry. I'm the only one getting therapy. Chances of him joining me are zero."

"Saying a few extra Hail Mary's couldn't hurt."

"You're right. Should I throw in a few Our Fathers for good measure?"

"You won't be throwing anything. With talk like that, the good Lord will turn a deaf ear."

"Sorry, Mom. I'll say some Glory Be's to make it up to you."

With a new school year approaching, Kate was busy buying supplies and new uniforms.

"I swear this process gets worse each year," she told Molly over lunch.

As she reached across the table for the breadbasket, Molly said, "Know what you mean."

In between mouthfuls of delicious warm bread and butter, Kate mumbled, "God, this is the greatest crusty bread. I could eat the whole basketful."

"You say that every time we're here," Molly said, handing Kate more bread.

"Because it's true. So...Anne can't find a backpack she

likes, and Mark only wants to use blue notebooks or folders. Both of them hate the new uniforms and Harry is no help. Keeps telling me, 'They're just kids. Lighten up.'"

"Lucky they're not in public school like my two. You'd be having the 'I'm not wearing this; it's scratchy,' or 'Everyone will laugh at this dopey sweater' fights."

"Yeah, but I have the Harry factor," Kate laughed. "He's been so crabby since Marcy's been gone."

"He should be happy he's got such a forgiving wife. I'd make his life miserable if I were you."

Kate eyed the remaining bread and reached for it, though she knew she'd be sorry when she stepped on the scale. "No. He swears he'll never hurt me like that again. I believe him. Don't know what made him get over his 'feelings,' but I'm guessing his meeting with the bishop might have had something to do with it."

Molly wasn't so sure. From what she'd heard and seen of Bishop George, he and Harry were a lot alike. Both men loved attention—whether it came from an employee or the Sunday congregation. She doubted George had had anything to do with Harry's decision to let Marcy go.

"Thinking this was just a bump in the road," Kate said, interrupting Molly's thoughts.

"Was it the long and winding road?" Molly blurted out without a second thought.

"Beatles. *Let It Be* album," Kate exclaimed, allowing herself to get caught up in the game—glad to shift the conversation away from Harry.

"Ah, you still got it! But I'm still ahead." Molly took a deep breath. "Kate, I just can't help wondering if Harry—"

"Do you know what I was wondering about the other day?" Kate cut in. "Jean Cohen. What happened to Jean

Cohen?"

"Your freshman roommate? She's probably president of some big company."

"You're probably right. Remember, she was a math major from some small town in Pennsylvania."

"Not quite the pocket-protector type, but oh my God, she was so organized."

"Insanely neat. Demanded lights out at nine p.m. Ten p.m. on weekends. A plotter with classes, meals, study time, and calls to her parents, charted on a wall calendar." Kate laughed. "Didn't own a pair of blue jeans, carried a briefcase to class, and always had an umbrella on her arm just in case the weather got ugly."

"You wanted to move out after a week of being told to pick up your clothes, make your bed, and straighten your desk."

"She was a bigger neat freak than my sister, Sue. We were in college, not the army," Kate lamented. "And your issues with your roommate, Judy Desale, were just as bad."

"All the same, from here on out she's 'Judy in disguise without glasses.'"

To which Kate responded, "John Fred and his Playboy Band."

"Not Gary Lewis and his Playboys, because 'everybody loves a clown,'" Molly shot back.

Having fallen back into their familiar college pattern, both Molly and Kate laughed, wistfully. *What if we could really go back in time?* Kate wondered. *What if I knew then what I know now? Would I have made the same choices?* Molly had kept a running count of who was on top. And though Kate was suspicious of Molly's calculations, as she was always one lyric or tag line behind, in the interest of friendship she'd let it go. Had she done the same thing with Harry all these years?

"It was such a relief second semester when I moved into your room, and Jean moved over to live with Judy."

"Yeah, but we still shared the same center room, though Jean and Judy refused to use it. They wanted nothing to do with us messy, boisterous Irish girls and our illegal beer in the fridge."

"If we played the stereo too loud, Jean pounded on the wall and yelled, 'Turn that down. People are trying to study.' Judy would do her one better and pull the plug."

"Remember when I was expecting a call from my mom, who was sick, and asked if they could answer the phone while I was in class? Judy and Jean said they would prefer not to."

"Who says something like that? 'I would prefer not to take your sick mother's call.'"

"I wanted to retaliate, short-sheet their beds and set their alarms for four in the morning. Mix their pencils in with pens and put Jean's books on Judy's desk and vice versa."

"Too bad they were in perpetual lockdown mode. They locked their bedroom door when they went to the bathroom and probably dead-bolted the suite door."

"We should have crawled in the window, like the boys did when they snuck in after hours."

"Yeah, but with our luck we'd get caught. End up at the dean's office, and our parents would have strangled us."

"Must be nice to have time for lunch with the ladies,"

Harry snidely remarked when he came home that evening. "I'm lucky I have time to eat an ice cream cone for lunch." Walking over to the dinner table, he stopped to give Anne a quick kiss on the top of her head and tousle Mark's hair.

"Don't mess with the hair," Mark said as he tried to restore order to his hair.

"Looks better now," Anne teased. Mark gave her a sneer and told her to shut up.

Kate interjected a stern, "Enough," and Harry laughed.

Picking up right where he left off, Harry sat down and said, "I have Bonnie doing some of Marcy's job, but need someone else to do the rest. My brother would be the logical choice, but I'm not sure he can handle more responsibility."

"Give him a chance," Kate said as she took the chicken tetrazzini casserole out of the oven. "You've said he's doing a great job with the stores he's managing. It'd take some burden off your back. Free you up for expansion," she added as she served up Anne's favorite dish.

"This looks great, Mom. I've been thinking about it all day. Kept me going through math class."

"You need more than chicken casserole to help you with your grades," Mark piped in.

"You're such a jerk," Anne countered.

"I know you are but what am I?" Mark shot back.

"You are sooo annoying, I—"

Once again, Harry laughed as Kate did the correcting. "Stop bickering."

With the children's war of words silenced, Harry looked over at Kate. "No offense, Kate, but getting back to the business of Press Agents, you've no idea how my business operates. You're a mom. Stick to do what you do best."

Kate fumed. When anyone disagreed with Harry, he went for the jugular. Kate was his latest victim. Seething, she looked down at her plate and said, "Of course," followed by a silent *fuck you.*

Why Harry felt the need to put her down in front of the kids, she wasn't sure. It left Kate wondering if she wasn't somehow to blame. She knew he was under a lot of pressure at work and maybe she was adding to it. Still, she wasn't happy with airing their differences in front of Mark and Anne.

She decided to let it go.

Chapter Seventeen

The next day, as he mulled over giving Steve more responsibility, his phone rang. He picked up the call and got a familial shove from his father.

"Heard you're sponsoring a tournament at the club. Business must be booming."

"Business is great, Dad. We're holding our own."

"Good to hear. You know, your mother and I've been talking about you giving your—"

Harry coughed, and coughed again. "Something in my throat. Need water. Hold on a sec."

Harry didn't need water. He needed time to calm down. He was angry. He knew instinctively that his parents were about to stick their noses into his business. But one deep breath later, he was back on the phone.

"Sorry. What were you saying?"

"No problem. So, remember your mother and I believed in you when you asked us for start-up money? You need to do the same for your brother. Give him more responsibility. He deserves it."

Gripping the sides of his chair, Harry was at the boiling point. Just as he was about to explode, his dad cut in with, "Offer him a small percentage of the company. A little insurance. Keep him invested in the business."

"I understand," he said. "I'll give him a call."

"Atta boy, Harry. He's family; he'll never let you down. Knew you'd do the right thing. Talk to you later."

Harry hung up the phone with steam coming out of his ears. Ready to explode, he yelled, "What?" when he heard a knock on his door.

"Nice—always answer a knock with venom in your voice?" Steve joked as he opened the door and came into the office. Harry reeled in his temper, leaned back in his chair, and smiled. "Perfect timing, was just going to call you."

Steve strode over to the chair in front of Harry's desk. "See? We're so close I can read your thoughts!"

Lucky for you, you're wrong, Harry thought, *or you'd know I'd like to clobber you. Same ole story, Dad is always looking out for you,* he mused as he shuffled the papers on his desk.

His brother had on one of his goofy smiles, and rather than telling him to lose the Cheshire Cat grin, Harry got down to business and offered him management of two additional stores.

"With a promise of reviewing ownership options in six to nine months."

"Why not now?" Steve shot back. "I can afford to buy in. It'd give you additional cash for expansion."

Harry chuckled. "I don't need your money. The banks have been more than willing to finance me in the past. I don't expect that to change."

"Okay. Didn't mean to offend you. What if we talk again in the fall? By that time, you'll see how well my stores are performing."

"Don't be so sure of yourself. Marcy's a hard act to follow. Managing two more stores won't be easy. Don't disappoint me."

"Yes, Master," Steve replied. He got up from his chair and bowed with praying hands. Harry ignored him. As Steve turned to go, he added, "You can be a real son of a bitch. Might come back to bite you."

"Thanks. I'll keep that in mind. Don't let the door hit you in the ass on the way out," Harry said, laughing.

In the next six months, Press Agents added two new locations and five commercial contracts. The two new stores were equipped to do some commercial cleaning, but not all, so Harry had to remodel two existing stores to accommodate the rest. As his accountant wasn't keen on Harry's taking on additional debt, he suggested that remodeling be delayed or at least kept to a minimum. "Buy used equipment and forgo some unnecessary updates," he advised Harry.

"I know what's necessary and what's not. As I've told you before, I understand what's best for Press Agents. Haven't been wrong yet. Thanks to me, your firm is doing very well."

Harry could almost hear his accountant take in his breath and hold it. He smirked. *Power really is an aphrodisiac*, he thought.

"Okay, just wanted to put it out there. I'm sure you're

right."

"I know I'm right. Oh, and get with the attorneys on setting up the new commercial cleaning corporation. They're dragging their feet. Find out what's taking so long."

"Of course. I'll do that when I hang up."

"I expect to hear from you by the end of the day."

The accountant hung up, wondering how Harry's wife could stand him. And maybe wondering why he didn't have the guts to fire him as a client. Or maybe, he just knew the answer and didn't even bother asking himself the question.

Harry's business sense had served himself and his family very well. So well that he surprised Kate with a double-strand diamond necklace on their fifteenth anniversary. Speechless over its sparkle, Kate gazed at it open-mouthed.

"It's stunning. The most beautiful necklace I've ever seen," she finally gushed.

"I thought so, too, but hold your applause. Your other gift isn't quite as grand."

Kate took the small, square box from Harry, thinking it was matching earrings. Opening it, she was transported into the nondescript coffee shop where they'd first met.

"Oh, Harry, this is so sweet," she said, staring down at the two Lincoln pennies. Overwhelmed by his thoughtfulness, tears came to her eyes.

"Didn't mean to make you cry," he said as a tear rolled down her cheek. "The dealer said they're each worth a few bucks more than the one-cent coins I dropped on the table when me met. So you got more than my two cents' worth in this marriage." He pulled her close and gave her a kiss. "You're still the one."

Tempted to revert to her game of song references, she almost blurted out, "Song by Orleans we played at our wedding reception." But warmed by the memory, she kept it to herself. "Thank you; I love you, Harry. You are so good to me."

Despite the last few years of a somewhat rocky relationship, Harry was still the one for Kate. She attributed his gift as an apology for the Marcy fiasco. His way of indicating that he, too, wanted to go back to the time they had met and fallen in love. She believed that, like her, he wanted to start over again.

Over the next few weeks, Kate's enchantment with Harry gradually subsided, then eventually crashed, leaving her feeling more desperate and angrier than before. There's something about hope being offered then retracted that cuts to the quick. Kate didn't love the workaholic Harry had become. He left for work earlier, stayed later, and never had time for lunch. She tried to revive old rituals, but when she asked if they could ever meet for lunch as they used to, he snapped, "I'm so busy I barely have time for a soda. Doing the best I can. You need to be more understanding." The happy anniversary haze was short-lived.

"Sorry. Feel like we hardly see each other anymore. I miss you. You're always so tired. Never have time to even throw the ball with the kids."

"Maybe you didn't hear me," he said impatiently. "I'm doing the best I can to keep you and the kids in the lifestyle you're accustomed to."

"We don't care about the lifestyle. We'd rather you were around more. We need more family time."

"Uh-huh. Hey, did you hear Michael Jordan made scoring history? Can't wait till we play the Bulls."

A few months ago, Kate would swear Harry wasn't with it. *Something's off*, she thought. She now knew differently. His annoying habit of changing the subject was not, as he had proclaimed, "Because my mind works faster than other people's."

It was a terrible excuse for not carrying on a conversation that he felt was finished, but the more Kate pointed it out, the worse it was for her. So, she learned to live with it.

Harry continued to work long days with little interest in romance. Their sex life was almost nonexistent. At first, Kate didn't mind the lack of intimacy. After running Anne and Mark to school or sports activities, doing laundry, and cooking dinner, she had little energy left. She tried working out harder with her trainer, but that only made her more tired. When getting more sleep didn't help, she asked Harry if he thought she might be sick, or as her mother often said, "coming down with something."

"No idea. See a doctor," he said, not looking up from his computer. As Kate walked over to see what he was so engrossed in, he closed the laptop. After a long sigh, he smiled. "With both kids in school all day, you should have enough time to relax. Wish I could do the same."

Wish you'd stop boo-hooing, Kate thought. Thankful he hadn't added something like, "How many women have a life as nice as yours?" she said nothing. She called the doctor and went in for blood work.

Chapter Eighteen

"Oh, dear God, you're kidding. How?" Harry asked with tears in his eyes. "Kate, what I meant was, how'd this happen?"

Kate's astonishment gave way to anger. "What do you mean how? I think you were there."

"I'm just surprised. When? We've hardly had..."

"Relations? Sex? Intercourse? Guess what? They are not dirty words. No trip to the confessional required."

Harry turned a faint shade of red and looked down. Kate felt sure he was horrified at her blurting it out. She was horrified by his tears.

"Why are you crying? I don't have cancer. I'm having a baby."

"Yes, yes, I get that. Need some time. Going for a ride. Be back by dinner," he said, picking up his keys and heading for the door.

Well, that went well, Kate thought as she watched him drive out. Angry at Harry's tearful reaction, she called her parents and sister.

"That's wonderful news! How are you feeling? Any morning sickness? Been to the doctor? When are you due?" Kate's mom fired off.

"I'm feeling okay. Been to the doctor. Don't have an exact date."

"Katie O'Brien! You've done this twice before. Must have some idea. Can't call Clare and Moira or Mrs. Casey with half the story."

Sensing her mom wasn't giving up, Kate told her, "About seven months from now. Any other questions?"

"My gran always said, 'No sense keeping your tongue under your belt.' Words I live by."

"You're doing her proud," Kate said before she hung up to call her sister.

After congratulating her and asking about her health, Sue added, "So, what really happened when you told lover boy he was going to be a dad again? There's more to this story."

Sue had a knack for spotting a watered-down version of the truth. Kate caved and told her everything, starting with his "How?" and ending with his tears.

"How? Didn't he get the 'this is how babies are made' talk? Never mind. Doesn't apply. Has two kids. He's one strange guy. Were they tears of happiness?"

"It was like his dog died. Said he needed time. Went for a drive an hour ago."

"Where'd he say he was going? Back for some priestly advice from the bishop?"

"Good God, I hope not. George is Harry's biggest fan. Still can't forgive him for telling Harry to explore his feeling with Marcy in the Bahamas."

"I can't believe Harry even told you about it. "

"I found it hard to believe when he told me. He made it very clear that he would have never gone because he valued our family so much. Said he thought George was just trying to help. Very 'priestly' of George."

"I'm sorry, Kate. I can't imagine how you must have felt."

"Thanks. I just want this whole thing to be behind us."

Back from his drive, Harry ran into Mark as he flew into the house through the open front door. "Hey buddy, what's the rush? Almost knocked me down."

"Sorry, Dad. Second time Mom called me for dinner. Don't want to get her mad."

"I hear you. I know how your mother gets. Let's not upset her," he quietly added as he followed Mark into the kitchen.

Dinner was Swiss steak, Harry's favorite. As he sat down, Harry looked around the table. "Where's the rolls?"

"In the trash. Burned to a crisp. Dinner was ready an hour ago," Kate said, steely-eyed.

Harry spooned out some mashed potatoes and turned to Anne. "So how was school? Need math help tonight? I was great in math."

Anne looked up from her plate and asked to be excused.

"I have lots of homework," she added as she pushed back her chair.

"You can wait till we are done with dinner," Harry said as he pointed at her.

"Harry, we're almost done and..." Kate stopped midsentence as Harry gave her a stern look.

Anne sat back down and Kate said nothing more.

"So...Mark, how's practice going?" Harry said, turning his attention to Mark.

Here he goes again, Kate thought as she pushed her Swiss steak aside. She hated Swiss steak almost as much as she hated Harry at that moment.

"Thought we were out of the baby business," Harry lamented to George over lunch at the club.

"Guess not. You two hadn't talked about this? No birth control?"

Squirming in his seat, Harry quietly said, "Thought she knew our family was complete. Figured she's older, and, well, she'd said she had early menopause, or something."

"Think she planned it?"

"Wouldn't put it past her. Now I'm stuck."

"Maybe not," George said thoughtfully. "You know, her age could be an issue. You wouldn't want a Down's syndrome baby. I'd suggest genetic testing."

"Yeah, good idea," Harry said as he ordered another drink.

When his drink came in a short glass with two lemons and not limes, Harry exploded.

"How hard is this?" he said to no one in particular. "I always order the same drink: vodka tonic, tall glass, two limes. Where's that nitwit waitress?"

"Right behind you, sir," the waitress answered curtly.

"My drink's wrong again," he said, whipping around in his chair. "This isn't rocket science. Probably is for you, though. Take this back!"

George laughed as the waitress picked up the drink.

That night, Harry broached the age issue with Kate.

Trying to keep from throttling him, Kate took a minute before saying, "I'm not as old as you."

"Isn't about me. You're the one having the baby. No sense taking a chance having a handicapped baby. Think genetic testing is a good idea."

"I don't. Wouldn't matter. Having the baby."

"Think about it, Kate. How hard it'd be on Anne and Mark."

"What I'm thinking about is going to bed. Not talking about this again. Get over it, Harry."

Abortion was not an option, and she wondered who had put the idea in Harry's head. She knew he'd met with the bishop, but surely a Catholic priest wouldn't suggest it. Or would he?

Stomping up to bed, Kate couldn't believe what her former altar boy husband was suggesting. She was sad he wasn't the man she'd once thought. It made her even more determined to love and care for this baby.

It took a few weeks, but Harry got used to the idea of becoming a family of five.

"Have no idea what's happened. But Harry's now the proud father-to-be," Kate told Molly. "I won't venture to guess what happened, but if I were you, I'd just go with it," Molly said. "Speaking of that, still planning to meet me and my roomies for beers and burgers?"

"I can do the burgers, but not the beer. What time?"

"Five-thirty work?"

"The old gals meet for the early bird special?"

"No way. You're the one who's pregnant. The rest of us are done having babies. We can stay up late. You can eat and go. We're allowed to stay out after dark."

Kate smiled, thinking how much she missed Molly and her other college friends. Harry had never liked any of their husbands, so they rarely got together. It'd be nice to laugh and go over crazy college memories.

"Oh, almost forgot to tell you," Kate said as she was about to hang up. "Bonnie, Harry's new Marcy, surprised him with the same news. She's been trying to have another baby for months. Harry's crazy happy for her. You'd think he was the father."

Molly paused, taking a second to think before answering, "Hope not."

Trying not to give Kate anything to worry about now, she added, with just a twinge of sarcasm, "Hey, maybe you and Bonnie can bond. Go shopping for maternity clothes together, compare diaper prices."

"Doubtful. That skinny little thing will be wearing tight little skirts the entire nine months. Harry said she's hardly showing. She'll probably gain a whopping ten pounds. I've packed that on and then some."

"Don't be so hard on yourself. I'm sure you look great."

"Give me another month, even my hair will be big."

Molly laughed. "That reminds me. My sister-in-law's nose grew when she was pregnant. Not a good look."

"Bet she didn't have in-laws pointing it out. Harry's dad's asked if I'm having twins, and his mom thinks my due date is off."

"Rough. What's Harry say about that?"

"Nothing. Claims I'm too sensitive."

"Imagine what he'd do if someone said he was a bit

tubby."

"Never happen. Weighs the same as when we met."

"Figures!"

On her way home, Molly thought about Kate's situation. Molly thought Harry's head was easily turned, but Kate had never seen it, and she had no intention of pointing it out. Even after his affair, Molly had avoided any Harry bashing. Wasn't her place.

"Those nine months flew by," Harry said to Kate between her contractions. They'd been at the hospital for an hour. Kate was becoming more and more uncomfortable. *Having a baby isn't for sissies*, she thought as a wave of pain rushed through her.

"Lucky you got a private room," Harry said as he walked around the bed. "Remember when you had Anne? Your roommate watched cartoons and sucked her thumb."

Kate nodded. The contractions were getting worse. Conversation with chatty Harry wasn't an option.

"Worse was when Mark was born," he went on. "That roommate was handcuffed to the bed. Remember, she named her baby Fee-malie."

"Don't care. Trying to breathe. So, so painful. This is the worst!"

"Said that with Anne and Mark. You lived through it."

Kate grunted. *If Harry doesn't shut it down, he won't live through this.*

Unable to read her mind, Harry kept going. "Know you like the name Emily for a girl, but reminds me of Emily

Byrd. Big tattletale in fifth grade. How about James for a boy? James Barny was an old neighbor. Drove a Harley. Envy of every kid in the neighborhood."

"Don't care. Need some ice chips," Kate said as she struggled to get comfortable.

"Okay. I'll find the nurse. Back soon," Harry said, hurrying out of the room.

"Don't rush," Kate said between grunts. If she'd had the strength, she would have cheered. Nothing like a break from chatty Harry.

He returned minutes later with a cup of ice chips and a newspaper. He handed Kate the cup of ice and sat down.

"Figured this'd take a while. Stopped for the paper. Want to check out our new ads. Should be in the second section," Harry said, opening up the paper.

Kate wasn't sure what was more annoying, his blabbering or the paper rustling. The pain was getting worse and her patience thin. *Enough*, she thought. *Dear Lord, get this baby out!*

"They're great!" Harry exclaimed, folding the page back. "Bonnie was right. Color adds a lot. Really pops. Want to look?" He inched over to her bed.

"No. Don't care about your dumb ad. Want this baby out! NOW!" Kate yelled.

Harry jumped back and grabbed a wet washcloth off the side table. "Take it easy, Kate," he cautioned as he wiped the sweat from her face. "Your blood pressure is going through the roof. Don't concentrate on the pain. Do those breathing exercises."

"Screw the breathing. Might be dying!"

"Don't think so. How about a little Father George humor? An Irish priest gets stopped for speeding. The trooper smells alcohol on the priest's breath and sees an empty wine bottle in the car. 'Been drinking?' he asks. 'Just water,' the priest replies. 'Then why do I smell alcohol?' Priest looks down at the bottle. Says, 'Good Lord, he's done it again!'"

Kate said between gritted teeth, "Old joke, Harry. Shut up!"

"Sor-ree. Won't say another word."

Good idea, Kate thought. *Men have been shot for less.*

Five hours later, their daughter Jamie came into the world.

Chapter Nineteen

Weighing in at over ten pounds, the blue-eyed, round-faced Jamie was the talk of the maternity ward. Surrounded by infants two to five pounds smaller, she looked three months older.

When Kate overheard another mother say Jamie looked big enough to wear shoes and carry a purse, she was horrified. After the woman's husband had added, "Wonder if she's potty-trained," Kate was ready to do battle. *How dare they*, she thought protectively, gazing down at Jamie's chubby little face. Images of Anne and Mark as babies floated through her head, and she quietly assured Jamie, "You're as perfect and beautiful as your sister and brother. The other babies here are scrawny."

When she'd told Harry what she'd heard, he laughed. "She's just a bigger bundle of joy. You're too sensitive. Besides," he said, with a forced smile, "probably has nothing to do with how much weight you gained."

Kate wrapped her arms around herself. Was she too

sensitive? That seemed to be the refrain whenever she expressed hurt in one form or another.

Was it better to keep everything in? Why would Harry mention her weight? He knew she struggled with it on a good day. How could he not know how much she was struggling the day after giving birth? Wanting to cry, she closed her eyes and tried to imagine herself fitting into her old jeans. It might take a small miracle and months of starvation, but she'd do it. She'd done it with the other two. She'd do it again.

Jamie's birth had left her feeling more drained and exhausted than she had after Anne's and Mark's. She just needed to get some sleep and wished Harry would leave. That didn't seem likely; he was glued to the chair and his *Wall Street Journal*. Harry would leave when he wanted and not a moment before. Resigned to his staying through the day, Kate's spirits were lifted when Anne sailed into the room. Clad in a coral angora poncho over beige pants and sweater, Kate thought she looked more beautiful than ever. Anne strode over to the bed with her distinctive perfume following in her wake.

Nodding to her dad, she sang out, "I know I was here yesterday, but I was missing Mommy and my new baby sister." Although she was a teenager, Anne was still comfortable occasionally calling her Mommy, and Kate loved it. Mark called it juvenile and countered by calling her Mother. Anne called her Mommy even more, just to annoy him.

She handed Kate a bouquet of pink daisies, just as Mark walked in. Dressed in blue crew-neck sweater and khaki pants, he looked like Harry's clone but with darker hair and green eyes.

"Flowers are from both of us—don't want Anne getting all the credit. Want my fair share," he said, grinning at his dad.

I wish I could bottle this happiness and use it when they're driving me crazy, Kate mused. She looked at her two older children and back at the flowers.

"You're both so good to me," Kate gushed as she smelled the flowers, and then set them on the night table. Anne leaned over the bed, gave her a quick kiss, and inched toward the bassinet.

"She's sleeping now," Kate softly told her, "but your little sissy was just asking about her big sister and brother."

"Of course, she was missing us." Anne picked up the tightly bundled Jamie and rocked her from side to side. Touching her little hands, she smiled down at her sister. "You're so beautiful, so perfect."

Mark came up behind her and whispered, "Don't be a baby hog."

"Back up. You'll get your turn!" Anne said with mock authority.

Listening to their banter filled Kate's heart with love and gratitude. It was the antidote to Harry's insensitive comments.

Jamie was a quiet, smiley baby who avoided the curse of colic.

"I knew she'd be a blessing," Kate's mom declared, hearing that Jamie had slept through the night by the end of her first month.

"She is a blessing. I'm always worried she might have health issues because of my age. My prayers to St. Gerard seem to be working. I think he watches over us and keeps her healthy."

"It's his job. He's the patron saint of mothers. Did the same for Sheila McCarthy. She had Maura in her late forties. She said she was the best of her lot."

Mrs. McCarthy's "lot" numbered nine, and Kate was pretty sure that by her ninth child, the woman might not have been of sound body or mind. That aside, she cheerfully said, "Remind me of that when Jamie's a teenager and we're fighting about curfew."

"There'll be no fighting, because as my own da told me, 'Right for me is right for you.'"

Knowing some things were sacred, Kate dared not laugh at her mom's reference to her grandfather. "I love her so much, Mom. She's such a happy, easy baby. I love having her all to myself after the kids leave for school."

"Not big on sharing?"

"By the end of the day, maybe. Mornings, no. I love sitting, holding her, and watching old *Andy Griffith Shows*. It's hard to beat a trip through Mayberry with Jamie."

"How's Harry doing?"

"Busy scouting new locations."

"Helping out at all?"

"More than with Anne and Mark. Got warming the bottle down to a science. Even changed Jamie's diapers— two were poopy."

"Thanks be to God and all his saints! He's helping out. How about Anne and Mark?"

"Love her to death. Always peering in the bassinet, fussing with her blankets, making sure she's okay. Last night, they tossed a coin to see who'd feed her. Anne won. Mark demanded a rematch."

Betty laughed. "Knowing Mark, I'm sure he'll get his fair share. By the way, your dad and I are planning on coming up Friday. It's supposed to get rainy in the afternoon, so we thought we'd leave early in the morning. Get there by lunchtime. Give you a break. You can get a nap in before Anne and Mark get home."

"Sounds great. You can hear all the lurid details of Anne's plan for sprucing up Jamie's wardrobe. She says Jamie needs to get out of one-piece sleepers and into little girl clothes. Wants to check out the latest baby fashion."

"I hope you don't let her talk you into buying one of those crazy baby headbands."

"That'll never happen. I remember when Mrs. O'Neil's granddaughter had one on and you asked her if she'd had surgery."

"As well I should have. I was ready to add the poor thing to my prayer list."

"I also know she hasn't talked to you since."

Breezing right over the memory, Betty moved on to her upcoming visit. "We'll call you when we leave, so if you need anything from the grocery store, we can stop on our way in. Oh, and Katie," she thoughtfully added, "enjoy these times. They're gone before you know it."

"Thanks, Mom."

Kate wished she'd listened to her mother. She had no idea then how quickly things would change.

Chapter Twenty

When Jamie became a toddler, her easygoing disposition took a U-turn. Prone to kicking and screaming when she didn't get her way, she wasn't easy to deal with. Calming her down took an enormous amount of restraint and patience. Kate had both. Harry had neither.

"She gets herself so worked up," Kate told her sister after one of Jamie's tantrums. "She kicks so hard I swear she'll break a foot. I thought she was going to kick out my car window when I told her we weren't stopping for ice cream yesterday. I'm trying to ignore it and let her work through it. Getting mad and yelling at her only makes it worse."

"Sounds like it takes the patience of a saint. Which reminds me, how is the sinner handling it? Meaning, of course..."

"Yeah, yeah, I got it. Harry has absolutely no patience with her, and she knows it. Gives him this low grunt when he gives her his 'knock it off' look. It makes me laugh."

"Bet Harry isn't laughing."

"No, it riles him that what worked on the other kids has no effect on Jamie. When she starts screaming, 'Go away, I want Mommy,' he's ready to explode. He says it's my fault she doesn't respect him, and I'm turning her against him."

"That'd be great if you had that power. Might serve him right."

"Serves nobody right. Why would I turn her against her own father? It's ridiculous. Harry's mom turned Harry and his brothers against their dad when he had his fling. It was a horrible thing to do. She convinced Harry and his brothers that talking to their father was taking his side. She played the 'poor me' card. Always making comments like, 'If your father hadn't abandoned us, this or that wouldn't have happened.' All of them bought it."

"I know; she's one tough nut, but Harry and his brothers were adults."

"They didn't act like it. They wouldn't answer their dad's calls and sent back the fruit baskets he sent them at Christmas. One time they all got together and ordered pizzas to his apartment. They thought it was hilarious. I never understood it. It was so heartless, especially since both of his parents had their issues. Don't get me wrong, I'm not saying her being hard to get along with justified his cheating, just that she had her part. It was a problem between two adults, and she shouldn't have dragged the kids into it. Lucky for his dad, he had the heart attack and everyone came to their senses. If that hadn't happened, they'd still be estranged."

"That's crazy. Who'd have thought trouble with your ticker could be a good thing?" Sue chuckled.

In an effort to understand Jamie's emotional triggers and keep Harry from boiling over, Kate decided to take Jamie to the pediatrician.

"I'm coming with you," Anne declared as Kate put Jamie's coat on. "I want to go to that cosmetic place in the same shopping center."

"For what?" Kate asked as Jamie tried to wriggle out of her coat.

"Stuff. I need new makeup."

"I really don't think—"

"I have my own money and checks."

"Checks?"

"Yeah, Dad opened a checking account up or me. I'll need it for college anyway."

Momentarily stunned and at a loss for words, Kate turned her attention back to Jamie.

"Get your coat, Anne, Jamie's on the run," Kate said in hot pursuit of Jamie.

Fuming that Harry had opened an account for Anne without telling her, Kate held her tongue. When they got to the doctor's office, Anne took off for the cosmetic store as Kate ushered Jamie in the waiting room.

"I want to make sure there isn't something else going on, like an ear infection," she told the doctor when he came in the examination room.

"Nothing I see," he said after a thorough examination. "She'll probably grow out of it."

"You said that about her eczema," Kate muttered

under her breath. She turned to the doctor and asked, "What do you suggest I do in the meantime?"

"Try giving her more choices. Make her feel more in control. Don't overstimulate her. Too much stimulation doesn't work for her sensitive personality."

And sometimes it doesn't work for mine, Kate ruminated as she shook the doctor's hand. She thanked him for his time and steered Jamie out the door to the car. Anne was waiting for them at the car with an oversized tote.

"What's with the giant bag? How much stuff did you buy? You can't possibly need—"

"Stop, Mom. It didn't cost you a thing. Take it easy," Anne said, putting on her headphones.

Buckling Jamie into her car seat, she kissed her on the head and squeezed her tiny hand. "You were such a good girl at the doctor's office. Daddy will be so happy to hear you were so grown up. Mommy loves you so much and is so proud of you."

Jamie smiled. Raising her hand to blow Kate a kiss, she said, "Love you too, Mommy."

Kate beamed. Jamie's simple words warmed her. "Love you with all my good heart."

As Kate pulled out of the parking lot, she remembered she had wanted to stop at Target.

"How 'bout we stop at Target?" she said as she looked in the rearview mirror at Jamie.

Jamie was staring out the window and ignored her. Kate upped the ante with, "You can get a yummy hot dog and a lemonade in a Little Mermaid cup."

A resounding "no" came from Jamie. Three kicks to the back of Kate's seat followed. *Here we go again*, Kate thought as she quickly put *101 Dalmatians* into the CD player.

"You need to get her under control," Anne said. "She's such a little brat."

"I'm trying," Kate said, waiting for the music to start.

"Listen Jamie, it's Pongo and Perdita! Everybody's going to the bow-wow ball, the big and small..." Kate sang out, glancing back at Jamie.

Jamie caught Kate's eye, smiled, and joined in singing, "Short and tall." A few notes later she was laughing, clapping, and shaking her head to the beat. Kate let out a long sigh of relief followed by a silent *Thank you, God!* Crisis avoided. One hot dog and half a cup of lemonade later, their Target trip was a success.

That night after Kate tucked Jamie in, she went back downstairs and told Harry the pediatrician's suggestions. He looked up from his newspaper and shook his head. "If you believe that mumbo-jumbo choice stuff, use it. She has to stop this. She's embarrassing. Never know what sets her off. Get her under control."

"You sound just like Anne, who by the way has a new checking account I knew nothing about."

"It's no big deal and don't make it one," Harry said as he dropped the paper and put his thumb and index finger together and pointed at her for emphasis.

Backing away, Kate retorted, "Please don't point at me. Its demeaning."

A slow smile spread over Harry's face.

"I'm working day and night for this family. You're pretty lucky, Kate. How many women—"

"Right, I almost forgot." Kate smacked her palm on her forehead and corrected herself. "Silly me." His pontificating was now beyond tiresome and had morphed into infuriating. She wanted to add what a big fathead he was, but, as always, decided against it.

American humorist Erma Bombeck once said raising a family wasn't something she'd put on her résumé, and she might not apply for the job again. After years of carpool, PTA meetings, bake sales, fundraisers, parent teacher conferences, and recitals, Kate was sure she would do it all again.

As she began cleaning up the house, she thought back on Anne's first day at preschool. She believed she'd be thrilled to have time to herself, but she'd come home and walked through the empty house feeling hollow. As she made the beds, she thought back on the nights she slept in Anne's twin bed after one of Anne's nightmares. Her back still ached when she thought of it.

When Mark went to school, it was worse. He spent the first two weeks crying at the classroom door. His teacher assured Kate he would get over it and suggested she give him her picture so he could pull his mom out of his pocket whenever he missed her.

When the picture idea didn't work, Kate contemplated pulling him out of school for a year.

Harry nixed the idea and told her "Mark needs to quit being a momma's boy."

With Jamie now in school, Kate couldn't help but feel her life was once again changing. Who was she without her children, she wondered as she heard the phone ring.

Running to pick it up, she was delighted to hear her mother's voice.

"So happy you called—I'm having a 'poor me, my kids are all grown up' day. I remember telling you I never had a moment to myself," Kate wistfully said as she threw Mark's sweaty gym clothes in the wash. "Hold on a minute, Mom. I have to turn on the washer before the gym clothes get up and walk away."

"Anne and Mark can't do their own laundry?"

"They can, but I don't mind doing it. It's no big deal, and not nearly as annoying as their inability to change out toilet paper rolls."

"Sounds serious," Betty deadpanned. "Part of raising three kids, and just when you've had enough, they grow up. Then you wish they were young again and miss all the craziness. It's a vicious cycle. My gran once told me having somewhere to go is home, someone to love is family, and having both is blessing."

"Makes sense. Harry's always said how blessed he is. I think he picked it up at one of his expensive dinners with George and those damn priests."

As soon as she'd said it, Kate knew she was in trouble. Damn and priests weren't two words Betty O'Brien would ever put together.

"Sorry, Mom. I shouldn't have said that about the priests. I really don't want to burn in hell."

"Apology accepted," Betty said with a sigh.

Life with strong, opinionated adult children could be trying, and Kate struggled to keep her Irish temper in check. Anne was twenty-two and working at Press Agents with her dad. Mark was twenty and finishing college. Both lived at home and spent more time telling her what she did wrong and less time asking for help. Harry, on the other hand, could do no wrong. What he said was law; what Kate said was up for discussion. He believed their children did little wrong and rarely supported Kate when she corrected them. When Harry agreed with Kate's corrections, he said nothing.

Kate had first noticed the change when the children became teenagers. Harry, the father who'd left child-rearing to Kate, morphed into Harry the overinvolved dad. He coached their games, took them golfing, and bought them tickets to concerts and sporting events. He was their biggest cheerleader and made sure he put it in writing. He'd leave small notes of encouragement in their rooms or tucked in their book bags. When they went off to college, he wrote them letters and followed up with twice-weekly phone calls. The kids loved his newfound attention and hung on to his every word. There was continual jockeying to win their father's approval and gain favor.

Harry played along, telling Anne she was his favorite one day, and Mark or Jamie the next. Kate remembered that Harry's mom had done the same thing to him and his brothers. She had thought it was a destructive game then and even more destructive now. When she mentioned it to Harry over breakfast, he said, "You just don't get it, Kate. I'm rooting for them; I'm always on their side."

"And I'm not?" Kate snapped back, looking up from her crossword puzzle.

Harry gave her a sad smile. "The kids and I think you're too hard on them."

Kate almost choked on her toast. "What?" she stammered, shoving her plate aside.

"I'm just saying, try to remember Anne's opinionated

and Mark's a young, cocky guy. Jamie's still young, but they're basically good kids. We're lucky," he said, dumping his half-eaten toast in the trash.

"Something wrong with the toast? Something else I need to 'work on'?" Kate asked, making air quotes for emphasis.

Harry walked over to her. He put his hands on her shoulders and calmly said, "Nothing is wrong with the toast. You need to—"

Not wanting to hear what else was wrong with her, she said, "So, for example, when Anne used the credit card to buy her friends drinks at a bar, that was okay cause she's a good kid? We agreed the card was only for emergencies."

"It was an emergency. The group was thirsty," Harry replied, laughing at his own joke. "You shouldn't have cancelled the card without telling her." He reached over to pick up his briefcase. "When it was declined, she was embarrassed."

"Tough. She knew the rules. She did it to herself."

"Says someone who doesn't always play by the rules. You'll regret your hard-nosed attitude. By the way, I got her another credit card," Harry said. Then, with an ever-so-slight smirk, he turned and walked out the door.

"You're rewarding bad behavior," Kate yelled after him. Furious that he'd gotten Anne another credit card behind her back, she was even more upset because he hadn't been supportive of her decision. They'd never even discussed giving Anne another card. What else had Harry done when she wasn't looking? Kate threw her half-eaten breakfast into the sink, turned on the disposal, and let it run for a good five minutes.

Chapter Twenty-One

Harry hadn't just changed his attitude about the children; he'd also changed his behavior toward Kate. He barely spoke to her before he left for work, and when he came home at night, he'd eat then fall asleep in his den watching the early news.

When Kate initiated conversation at the dinner table, he'd turn and talk to Jamie. Kate tried cutting in with some innocuous news of her day, but Harry would either resume eating or simply not respond. She didn't understand it and didn't like it. He wasn't nasty, he just didn't engage. She was the odd man out.

Troubled by it all, she somehow pushed away her fears and anger, as she usually did, and focused on the positive. At least he was finally over his "Jamie likes you better" attitude.

The problem was that Harry didn't appear to like Kate any better, even though she tried damn hard to appease him. Years later, she would tell her sister that she always thought if she danced a little faster or jumped a little higher, everything with Harry would be better. It was a pipe dream, but one Kate held fast. Harry, however, did not and had no interest in either talking to her or having sex with her.

Kate thought his performance—or lack of it—was an issue that embarrassed him. She'd have been happy if he'd shown her affection in other ways, but he didn't. She still loved him, despite his indifference toward her, and she believed he still loved her, though she wasn't quite sure what that meant anymore. She couldn't imagine Harry leaving her for someone else. Still, she wondered if he was showering someone else with the affection he withheld from her.

Her first guess was that Bonnie, who had taken over for Marcy, had taken over Harry as well. He'd never gushed over Bonnie as he had Marcy, but he might have learned to keep his mouth shut. If not Bonnie, then who? Kate began wrestling with the idea that Harry was cheating again and decided she had to know for sure.

Returning to her middle-of-the-night sleuthing, she checked his sports coat pockets and went through his briefcase. Nothing. A search of his desk drawers and car yielded the same results. Relieved she had found no incriminating evidence, she began to think it was all in her head.

But when Harry came home with a half dozen new, silk boxer shorts he said he'd bought at the outlets, Kate was certain she wasn't imagining anything. Harry had never shopped at the outlets, nor worn silk underwear. Not knowing what to say and not wanting to cry, her dilemma was solved when he looked her straight in the eyes and said, "Read somewhere boxers help with things."

She almost blurted out, "You've worn boxers before and they didn't do the trick." Instead, she stared at the garish silk boxers and wondered what he'd been reading. Sounded like something that had come from a magazine hidden under an adolescent boy's mattress.

Kate wanted to believe him, but weeks went by and the boxers performed no magic. Disheartened, she hit a new low when she found a bottle of blue pills hidden in the back of his file drawer. It was a performance-enhancing drug. And he obviously wasn't taking it for her. Closing the drawer quickly, as if she could block out the image, she decided she'd wait to see what would happen next.

Two days later, after Harry had left for work, she rechecked the drawer. The bottle was gone. Did he know she'd gone through his drawers? How could he? He had been sleeping when she'd found the little blue pills; how would he have known? Looking over at his laptop, she panicked, wondering if the computer's camera had recorded her. If that was even possible.

Kate wondered if Harry had an app on his phone that had accessed his computer's camera. If so, Kate assumed someone else must have downloaded it for him because he wasn't tech savvy. Bonnie had handled the company's computer work in the past, but Harry had said Kellie had updated their systems. According to Harry, Kellie was a computer whiz and a wonderful asset to his growing business. Bonnie had brought her on board, and Harry's praise sounded eerily similar to that of Bonnie and Marcy before her. Was history repeating itself? Which one of them had helped him?

I'm really making myself crazy over all of this. I'm sure

there is some logical explanation. I just need to calm down, take a breath, stop being as nutty as Harry says I am.

Trying to sort it out, Kate was startled when the doorbell rang. She opened the door and was surprised to see her sister.

"It's only ten. I thought we're meeting Mom and Dad at noon."

"We are," Sue said as she walked into the house and took off her coat.

"Mom and Dad okay?" Kate asked as they moved into the kitchen.

"They're fine."

"Pete and the kids?"

"Fine too," Sue said with a long sigh. She looked around the kitchen, then focused back on Kate.

"What?" Suddenly aware of Sue's scrutiny, Kate added, "I haven't picked up the breakfast dishes, so it's a little messy in here." Looking down at her baggy sweats and ratty T-shirt, she felt as messy as her kitchen. "And I haven't taken a shower or washed my hair yet, so..."

"You look fine," Sue said and paused as a nervous Kate cut in.

"What's going on? Why are you here?" Her heart rate increased, as did her volley of questions. "Did you see Harry out with some girl? Last weekend when I was at Mom and Dad's? Someone else see him? Think he's up to his old tricks? He is. I found evidence."

"Calm down. Let me explain," Sue said in a soothing voice as she wandered around the kitchen.

Kate tried to calm down by taking a swig from her half-empty water bottle. She knew she had been rambling, and when she saw the pained look on her sister's face, she felt a stabbing pain at her temple.

"Okay if I grab a water from the fridge?" Sue suddenly asked, scurrying over to the refrigerator.

"Sure," Kate said as her throbbing headache intensified. Her sister was stalling.

"So..." Sue began slowly as she closed the refrigerator door. "Pete ran into Harry and Bishop George on the golf course. They had a beer together."

"And?" Kate asked in a high-pitched voice. She said a fast prayer, steeling herself for what was to come.

Her sister did the same. This wasn't going to be easy for either of them.

"Harry told him he and the kids are worried about you," Sue mumbled, twisting off the top of the bottle. She took a slow drink and leaned against the counter. "He said you haven't been yourself lately. Impatient with the kids. Always angry and accusing him of cheating. Thinks you're drinking too much."

Kate was angry, but also horribly hurt. "You believe him, don't you? You think I've lost it. Just a crazy drunk!"

"I didn't say that. I just wanted to let you know, be sure."

"Sure, about what? That I'm not tipping a few at ten a.m.?"

"That's not it at all, Kate."

"Then what?" Kate jumped up out of her chair.

"You're taking Harry's side, aren't you?" Kate spat out. "He's turning my kids against me, and you and Pete are cheering him on." She pitched her water bottle across the room.

Taken aback by Kate's sudden outburst, Sue looked at Kate wide-eyed. "I'm sorry," she said, trying to put her arms around her sister. "I'm not trying to hurt you. You've been through a lot. I know it's been tough."

"No, you don't know. No one does." Kate pushed her sister away. "I'm always looking over my shoulder, wondering who he'll bed down next."

"He said he's changed; any proof he hasn't?"

Not willing to share her suspicions with someone she believed was on Harry's side, Kate held her tongue.

"I'm so sorry, Kate. I love you. I only want to help."

Too upset to say any more, Kate pointed to the door. Sue tried to put her arms around Kate again, but Kate shook her off. "Get out," she hissed.

Sue picked up her coat, opened the door, and looked back at Kate. "No one's against you. We all love you. I'll always be here for you."

"Tell Mom and Dad I'm sick," Kate said bitterly as she banged the door closed.

As soon as the door slammed shut, the tears Kate had been holding in sprang out. She pounded on the door, sobbing and yelling at God for abandoning her. Her world was crumbling, and she had no tools to stop the destruction. Everyone was against her.

She grabbed some tissues from the bathroom and marched up to bed. Maybe she'd fall asleep and never wake up. While she was angry with her sister for buying Harry's story, she was even angrier with herself for falling in love with such a heartless liar. For still loving him, despite everything.

After she'd tossed and turned for over an hour, she gave up trying to fall asleep. Without thinking, she walked into Harry's closet and studied his designer suits still hanging in their dry-cleaning bags. She touched one of his button-down shirts, lined up by color—all the blues together, all the whites together. She felt sick with anger and reached into her dresser drawer for a pair of scissors. She could cut up every suit and every shirt and toss them out the window. But Harry would just replace them, and it would be another strike against her. Besides, Jamie had to be picked up at two. And Jamie was still on her side. Jamie loved her and believed in her.

Kate slammed the closet door shut and checked her watch. She still had two hours. The more she thought about her mess of a life, the angrier she became. Time to flip into crisis mode: extreme cleaning.

She washed the first-floor windows, dusted the baseboards, vacuumed, and cleaned out the refrigerator. She finally wrapped it up after cleaning her closet.

Satisfied she'd done something positive, she got into the shower, hoping to wash away the pain inside her. Standing under the warm water calmed her, but her mind was racing. She'd gone from wondering about Harry's pill stash to worrying about losing her mind. Why had Harry said those things about her? Why did her sister believe him? Did her kids think she'd gone mad? Was all this her fault?

Chapter Twenty-Two

Kate's mother had often encouraged her to "take the bull by the horns" when faced with difficult situations. It was time to do that with Harry and his blue pills. On Saturday afternoon, after Anne and Mark left with Jamie to go to a basketball game, Kate seized the moment. Her heart was thumping in her chest and her hands were clammy. Harry was her husband; she shouldn't be nervous. She loved him, and he loved her. But why had he hidden the pills?

Feeling she needed to get rid of her nervous energy before talking to Harry, she mopped the kitchen floor, unloaded the dishwasher, and took out the garbage. Ready to tackle the laundry, she stopped midway up the stairs when she heard Harry coming down the hall.

"Pretty quiet around here," he said, strolling into the kitchen. Kate turned and walked back downstairs.

"Yeah. Nice of Mark and Anne to take their little sister to the game." She followed Harry over to the refrigerator.

"Jamie really looks up to them, and they are so patient with her. Anne even suggested they bring one of Jamie's middle school friends along."

Opening the refrigerator door, he reached for a bottle of grape pop and took a gulp. "I always took my younger brothers to games. They loved it. We had some great times."

"I remember Steve talking about that last Thanksgiving," Kate added as Harry put his pop back in the refrigerator.

"Harry," she began, "I, ah, need to talk to you."

"Well, that doesn't sound good. What is it?"

When she told him she'd found the pills, he said nothing. Not knowing what else to say she took a deep breath and waited.

"Oh Katie, I've been taking pills on and off for the past few months. You kept complaining about how I'm not there for you, so I decided to try something to solve it. Funny thing is they have an interesting side effect; I have more energy. I feel better, particularly when I work out—especially when I run."

Kate stared at him, dumbfounded. Had he really just told her the pills helped him run better? She was confident it wasn't a side effect she, or any rational person, had ever heard of. Did he think she'd buy it? Obviously so, because he smiled patronizingly and said, "I love you, Katie." Then he patted her on the head and strutted out of the kitchen.

Katie? Where did that come from. He had played her for a fool, and she was livid. She wanted to scream at him, but knew she'd also be tempted to slap him across the face. Hard. It would be cathartic, but he'd use it against her with the children. Better to calm down.

It was close to five somewhere in the world. Time for the balm of alcohol. She poured herself a generous glass of wine and went out to sit on the patio. It was a warm fall day and Kate found some peace watching the squirrels chase each other and the birds swoop into the bird feeder. Life in nature was going on as it should, and it gave her comfort that hers could do the same.

Harry spent the rest of the afternoon in his den doing paperwork. Kate, determined to keep her cool, poured out the last of her wine, combed her hair, tucked in her shirt, and strode into his den.

"I was thinking we could get Chinese food for dinner. Not sure when the kids will be home, so it would be easy."

"Sounds good," Harry answered as he quickly closed his laptop. "Do something different with your hair?"

"Just combed it."

"Oh, didn't mean to offend you. Looks good. Is that the sweater I gave you? Looks nice on you. You should wear it more often."

They were small compliments, but they made Kate feel better. It gave her hope that things would be okay between them. She'd probably look back on this all and laugh.

Before she could thank him, Harry switched gears.

"Your car lease is almost up. I'll meet you at the Auto Mile tomorrow to look at new cars. See what you like."

Once again, Kate was taken by surprise. She almost asked if he planned on running to the dealership or driving over. *Most likely drive*, she thought, *performance enhancers probably have a mileage limit.*

"Yeah, sure," she said. Wanting to put an end to the rumblings in her heart, she thought about pleading with Harry to level with her. She settled for a silent, *Whatever.*

The next day, true to his word, Harry met her at the Auto Mile. They looked at a variety of sedans and SUVs. Kate liked them all, but was partial to a mint-green SUV.

"The lease will be more than what you're paying on your car now," Harry said as he looked over the paperwork. "Trust me, you can't afford it. Already give you my whole paycheck. Can't do any more."

"Okay, forget the SUV," Kate said, realizing she couldn't afford a bigger car payment. She was still paying off her credit card bills from Christmas, and that was three months ago. When she had asked Harry for more money at Christmas, he had given her the same, "Give you my whole paycheck; there is no more," line. She knew there was more money somewhere, because he had his own checking account and paid his own credit card bills. But it didn't seem worth getting worked up about a car, so Kate reluctantly accepted his "can't squeeze blood out of a turnip" excuse. There were other, more pressing issues to be upset about.

Kate settled on another station wagon. Two weeks later, Harry drove home the same green SUV she had wanted, having leased it for himself. Years later, when she thought about the car incident, she recognized how blatantly self-centered Harry had become and how unimportant she had become—to him and to herself.

"It's a business expense," he had explained. "Besides," he tousled her hair, "a station wagon is a better fit for you."

Better how? Kate fumed. Anne and Mark had their own cars, and Jamie was three years away from getting her license. Station wagons were for moms with a carload of kids. She was well past that stage and well past believing in Harry.

Anne and Mark not only believed in their dad, they worshipped him. Jamie, Kate feared, would soon follow suit. Kate was tolerated and often the odd man out. It was Harry and the older kids who skied the black diamond runs in Telluride, while Kate struggled alone on the blue hills, occasionally joined by Jamie after ski school. She didn't like heights, and flying down a steep hill with two sleds on her feet terrified her. Harry had told her she needed to challenge herself. To stop being a baby. Mark and Anne had laughed and agreed. Mark had even suggested she join Jamie at ski school.

"She's too old for my class," Jamie said, much to the delight of her sister and brother. Harry laughed and said beginner ski classes weren't a bad idea.

When Kate refused them anything, Harry would swoop in and override her decision. His override often had a "you know how your mother is" tagline attached. When Anne wanted a to move to from her apartment to an expensive condo, Harry was ready with a blank check. A new Audi SUV came Mark's way after he complained his jeep was noisy and drafty.

She didn't approve of giving into the children's every whim, but when she complained to Harry he'd said, "You are too hard on them, and don't understand them as well as I do."

Kate would end up in tears, and Harry ended up being the good guy. She had often heard him tell the kids, "Your

mom's having some hard times. Let's leave her alone."
That's exactly what they did.

Kate had become invisible.

"Don't know what's wrong with me. I'm always so sad," she said to Molly when they met for a walk in the park. When Molly said nothing and picked up her pace, Kate matched her step for step. "Harry said the kids told him I need medication. Hey, if you don't slow down, I may need heart medication," she said, puffing.

Molly laughed. "So, what did you say? Do you believe him?"

"Hard for me to believe my kids would say that, but I won't ask them. I don't want to put them in the middle."

"Harry knows that. Don't believe his bullshit," Molly shot back.

"But what if I am the problem? Am I making everyone miserable?"

"No. You are making yourself miserable, and Harry's adding fuel to the fire. He's Mr. Big Bucks. He thinks his money has made him smarter and better than the rest of us mortals. Unfortunately, he may be convincing your kids of that."

"And my sister. We're barely speaking."

"She told me. Ran into her after mass. She asked if I'd seen you and said she regrets telling you what Harry had said. You should call her. Set her straight. I know she misses you."

"Suppose so," Kate answered, wondering what else Molly and Sue had talked about. Did they think she was on edge? Or on the edge of the bridge? Pushing it all to the back of her mind, she said, "My mom's been bugging me about why Sue and I aren't speaking."

"Your mom's sharp. She knows it has something to do with Harry."

"Doesn't everything have something to do with Harry?" Kate said, disgusted, as they completed their four-mile speed walk.

"Seems like it," Molly said over her shoulder as they crossed the grass to the parking lot. "Don't let him drag you down. He wouldn't be where he is today without you."

Kate chuckled. "It's not me. He swears it's his determination and commitment. Told the kids he can do anything he sets his mind to. No limitations."

"A bit narcissistic, wouldn't you say?"

"I would and I do. I can't imagine how it will be when Jamie's gone and we're empty-nesters."

"Ever think of separating for a while?"

Kate took a minute before she responded, "I've thought about it. I know I need a break in the action, but don't know where I'd get the money."

"You're married to the king of the dry-cleaning world and you're worried about money?"

"I am. I can't pay off my charge accounts, and Harry won't help. He said I already get more money than any of our friends."

"He knows that how? Kate, this may sound harsh, but it's time Harry gets a kick in the ass. Get away from the bastard for a while. I'd gladly give you a loan."

Chapter Twenty-Three

Kate appreciated Molly's offer but ended up not needing a loan. Harry gave her a check that he'd said "should easily cover your living expenses until you get it together and come back."

As much as she hated saying it, Kate thanked Harry and sarcastically added, "I appreciate your cooperation." *What a load of crap*, she thought after she said it. What she'd appreciate was a partner who was a faithful husband. That wasn't Harry. She didn't want to break up the marriage, but she was tired of sharing her husband with his coworkers. A separation had saved Harry's parents' marriage. Why wouldn't it do the same for theirs?

Confident it was the right thing to do, she decided to tackle the next hurdle—telling Jamie, their only child still at home. Nervous about how she'd react, Kate chose her words carefully.

"I need some time to get back to being me, and I think a separation from your father is the best way to do that.

We're not getting divorced, just taking a time-out. You'll live with me but be able to come back here whenever you want. We both love you and want to do what's best for all of us. I'm sorry it's come to this, but—"

Jamie interrupted Kate and took her hand. "It's okay, Mom. I get it. There's been too much drama going on. I'm tired of it. We'll be fine."

"Of course, we will. This is just a temporary thing. That's why I think—"

Jamie jumped in. "I want to take all my stuff and don't want to change schools. Hope you didn't pick out some crappy place. I need my own bathroom and space to have friends over."

Kate stifled a laugh over Jamie's "all about me" attitude. Jamie was a bona fide teenager.

"It's a three-bedroom townhouse in that new development near your school. We'll have our own garage and a small backyard," Kate said, relieved Jamie seemed okay with moving.

Jamie smiled and looked down at her phone.

"Yeah, whatever," she said. "Maureen and MaryAnn want to go to the basketball game. Can you drive? Maureen's mom will pick up."

"Sure, glad to," Kate responded. As Jamie bounded up the stairs to get ready for the game, Kate sat in stunned silence. Jamie was okay with the move. *It's a new adventure*, Kate thought as she dialed Molly's number. Molly answered on the first ring.

"So, how'd it go? Jamie okay?"

"Went over better than I thought it might. She's such a great kid, such a joy to be around. She gives me so much strength. Couldn't do this without her. I know it can change in a minute. Moms and teenage daughters aren't known for always seeing eye to eye."

"Amen. You're preaching to the choir. My Mary's singing that same ole song."

"But with a different meaning. Four Tops," Kate said, back in their college game that made the world seem a tiny bit brighter.

When Kate told her parents over dinner that she and Harry were separating, they weren't surprised.

"We know you've been unhappy and struggling to keep it together," Betty said as she put down her fork, giving Kate her full attention. "Maybe some time away will help. Gives Harry a chance to get back to his old self." She reached for Kate's hand across the table.

It was a small, sweet gesture, and Kate smiled at her mother's kindness. "Not sure he can do that." Tears unexpectedly filled her eyes. She wanted to be brave in front of her parents and was nervous they would think less of her for leaving.

"I know it's best for me and for Jamie," Kate said, struggling to sound confident. "I need to get her away from Harry's influence, or I'll lose her, too. Anne won't take my calls, and Mark's assistant keeps telling me he's busy and will call later. Never does. Even tried talking to his crazy wife. At least she took my call. But then she says, 'No idea why you'd leave. You could have bought anything you wanted.'"

"'Better to be a woman of character than a woman of means,'" Betty said, referring to an old Irish proverb. "Mark and Anne are hurting, but you haven't lost them, and you won't lose Jamie. You're their mom; you gave them life. I can't imagine Harry wanting the children estranged from their mother."

Kate was tempted to say, "That's exactly what Harry wants. He's following in his mother's footsteps. He knows how much it hurts me. That's his plan." And although she believed it was true, she wasn't sure she should say it out loud. What if this was all in her head and a separation straightened things out? She believed she could forgive Harry, but she wasn't sure he'd forgive her for leaving.

"I'm just telling the kids I need some time away. They don't need to know their dad's a habitual cheater."

"I can appreciate you wanting to protect your children, but they're adults," Betty said. "Aren't they mature enough to handle the truth?"

"Kids never want to know their parent has committed adultery. Plus, what if things work out and we get back together? It happened with Harry's parents. I don't want them to always think of him as a cheater."

Betty and Ed respected their daughter's decision but were against her shouldering the blame. Sensing Kate was determined, they reluctantly opted to give her their support about this aspect of the separation.

"We'll always be here for you and Jamie and Anne and Mark," her dad piped in. Then, balling his fists, he said, "I've half a mind to give Harry a good talking-to. Pound some sense in him."

"You'll do nothing of the sort. A silent mouth is melodious," Betty chastised.

Ed gave her a low grunt, and Kate covered her mouth to keep from laughing out loud. Her parents' back-and-forth amused her. Their words were never laced with spite or anger. It was something she and Harry had lost long ago.

"Know that we love you and believe in you," Ed said, relaxing his hands and moving over to Kate with open arms. He hugged her and kissed her hair.

Betty grinned. "It will all work out with Harry, Katie. Have...have you worked things out with your sister?" she asked, hoping it didn't sound as if she were making a suggestion. She knew no matter how she asked, Kate knew her well enough to understand it was just slightly lower down on the scale than an order. As far as Betty was concerned, the eleventh commandment was "Thou shalt respect family ties under all circumstances."

She was relieved when Kate answered her in the affirmative. "Yes. I bit the bullet and went over to let her know what's really been going on. She was amazed and even apologized for believing this was all about me, for thinking Harry was an innocent bystander."

"There are always two sides to every story. Harry can be convincing. He didn't get to where he is by accident."

"Yeah, he constantly reminds me of that and how ungrateful I am," Kate said. "Always telling me I'm not thankful enough for all he's given me. Seems to have forgotten I once had a job..."

"And a good-paying one at that! He's a phony baloney! Wouldn't be where he is without you behind him. Don't forget that, Katie."

Kate smiled. Warmed by her parents' love and confidence, she said, "Love you both."

But as she drove away from their protection, the bile of unrecognized regret coursed through her stomach and into her mouth. If her mother was right—that there were always two sides to every story—what was Harry's side? What had she done to make him cheat on her?

Initially outraged by Kate's separation suggestion, Harry warmed to the idea after discussing it with George.

"What kind of mother leaves their children?" George asked Harry when they met for drinks at the club. "I know Anne and Mark are married and on their own, but Jamie's still home."

"She said Jamie's moving out with her."

"And you're okay with that?" George downed the last of his cocktail and signaled the waitress to bring another round.

"Not really, but my attorney said that since Jamie's under eighteen, I can fight for custody if we divorce."

"Glad you got an attorney."

"Figured I had to. Kate's no dummy; she'll interview all the top divorce attorneys first, just so they can't take my case."

"Probably. Actually, this might be a good thing. Gives you more time with Bonnie. Don't know how you've kept it from Kate. Guess you had a little previous experience with Marcy."

"This time it's even easier. Kate may be suspicious, but she has no idea what's going on. Bonnie and I meet up at different hotels and only at lunch. It works. Thing is," Harry stopped to let the waitress set down his new drink, "Kate hasn't been a bad mother until this point. I've just moved beyond her. Don't love her anymore. And I don't believe she will actually move out when it comes down to it. And I really don't want her to. I like things just the way they are."

"She's a bit dramatic. Even if she does move out, she'll be back home in no time," George reassured Harry. "Enjoy the break. But I'd hold off on any Press Agents expansion plans till you see how this goes."

"Agreed," Harry said, chewing on the ice from his drink.

"Harry, you don't think..." George began. Then he took a small sip of his drink. His eyes were slightly averted.

"Don't think what?"

"Kate doesn't know about what happened to you..."

"In high school? Not unless you moved to the other side of the confessional box."

"Just a bit worried. I only want the best for you," George said solemnly as he reached across the table and patted Harry's hand.

Looking down momentarily, Harry pulled his hand back and flinched. "You've always been a great friend, George. Can't thank you enough."

"Sure, you can." George reached into his pocket for a set of papers. "I want to update the rectory. Feels like I'm living in a house from the 1950s."

Harry leafed through the papers and pushed them back across the table to George.

"You never cease to amaze me," he said, shaking his head at his old friend. He reached into his pocket and took out a pen and his checkbook. In quick succession, he wrote out a check, handed it to George, gulped down his drink, and tossed his napkin on the table. When he pushed his chair back, George understood their conversation was over.

He folded the check and put it in his pocket. "More

than generous. Thank you, Harry."

On their way out, Harry stopped to talk to an older man two tables down.

"Good to see you, Bob," he said, carefully shaking the man's frail hand. "How's Doris? Heard she had a bad fall."

"Fell down the three stairs going into our garage—broke her glasses, cut her face, and sprained her ankle."

"So sorry to hear it. I'm sure you're taking good care of her."

"Trying to. She's at home resting, so I came to meet the other old-timers for lunch."

Harry chuckled. "Hey, you can still hit a damn long drive. Hear Mike Collins is a few bucks down after your last match."

"You're a sharp one, Harry. Always on top of things. Thanks for asking about Doris. I'll tell her I saw you."

Harry patted him on the back and turned to leave just as a dark-haired beauty came out from behind the bar. Harry smiled at her and nodded his head. She did the same.

George caught the gesture and laughed. "You still got it, Harry."

"That I do," Harry replied.

Chapter Twenty-Four

When Kate moved to the condo with Jamie, she thought it the best solution to possibly saving her marriage and her sanity. Harry's snide and angry comments were tearing her apart. Regaling her shortcomings was commonplace. If he wasn't making a dig at her, he was silent. He rarely spoke to her at dinner, and if Anne and Mark were at the table he didn't speak to Jamie. Jamie, Kate knew, felt snubbed and took to humming at the dinner table.

"Sometimes I think I'm overreacting. I get so mad at him and come back with a snarky comment and then he calmly tells me he loves me," Kate told her psychologist. "I know you say it's passive-aggressive behavior, but I must be doing something to bring it on."

"Don't engage," the doctor told her. "Walk away or hang up the phone. Don't respond."

Keeping her mouth shut was becoming harder and harder, and she felt being apart from Harry would save her from herself.

What little hope she had for a peaceful separation was dashed soon after the move. Harry, who demanded to drive Jamie to school two days a week, wouldn't come to the door to get Jamie.

"It's so hurtful that you've moved away from the family. You've taken Jamie away from her sister and brother," Harry declared one morning as Kate walked Jamie out to the car.

"Anne and Mark are adults, living on their own. They have cars and can easily come over and see their sister. They are always welcome here."

"They're mad, and embarrassed. They don't want to be a part of this pain you are causing," Harry responded in a soft and soulful voice. "The children and I think you need to get it together and come home. Back where you belong."

Unwilling to grill Anne and Mark about Harry's comments, Kate never knew if what Harry said was true. Anne and Mark were happy to see Jamie but only at Harry's house. They never came to Kate's; yet when she'd dropped Jamie at Harry's, they acted like nothing was wrong. Days later, they wouldn't answer her calls or texts.

Kate assumed they needed time to adjust and that their anger and bitterness would subside, but it only intensified.

Mark told Kate she had humiliated their father and she needed professional help. He also suggested she take $50,000 and just move away—out of the city.

"Fifty thousand dollars? You're joking, Mark. Where will that get me?" Kate asked. Mark hadn't answered, just hung up the phone. Horrified her own son would suggest such a thing, she was equally shocked when Anne told her she'd never forgive her for turning her back on their father. He'd worked so hard and she was never thankful for all he'd done for her, Anne had added.

Kate prayed that time would heal their wounds, but God turned a deaf ear. Though she was thankful she had Jamie, she missed Anne and Mark, missed hearing about their busy lives and growing careers. She wondered if Anne was still seeing that nice guy Joe from New Jersey or if Mark liked working for his father. The more she wondered, the more she convinced herself she must be doing something wrong.

What little Kate did hear about her older children, she heard from other people. One day a former neighbor congratulated her in the grocery store. Not knowing why or what had happened, Kate said a quick thanks and left the store shaking with anger. What happened and what didn't she know?

Texts to Anne and Mark went unanswered. She'd have to call Harry.

"What's happened, Harry? Why did Sara Olsen congratulate me in the grocery store?" Kate demanded when Harry came on the line.

"Oh, thought she'd tell you, but you know you did abandon them...and..."

"Harry, please, what is going on?"

A short sigh and a quick clear of his throat and Harry blurted, "Anne and Joe are engaged. Getting married in six months."

If that wasn't enough to break her heart, Harry added, "I'm sorry the kids don't have a relationship with you. That's their decision, nothing I can do about it. And Kate, Anne doesn't want you at the wedding. That might be hard for you, but..."

Chocking on her tears and unable to respond, Kate hung up.

She wanted to call Anne and Mark and tell them she suspected Harry had been cheating on her for years, but she knew they'd never believe her. She had no real proof since his Marcy dalliance, and the detective she hired to follow him gave her nothing but a $1,500 bill. The longer they had been separated, the worse things had gotten. Harry wasn't getting any easier to get along with and she worried he was putting pressure on Jamie to move back in with him. The longer it dragged on, the likelier she was to lose Jamie too. It was time to separate herself permanently from Harry.

Divorce is never easy on a family, but Harry made sure theirs was devastating. Though Kate had physically left the house, he'd left the marriage years before. In Harry's world, however, that was immaterial. The fact that Kate had moved only a mile away—and that Harry had written the check allowing her to move out—never entered the equation. The family had broken up because "Kate abandoned her children." He not only declared that to be true, but also reinforced it with tears and wailing and gnashing of teeth at their final divorce hearing. Rolling her eyes at his performance and ready to tell him to knock it off, Kate caught her attorney's stern look and said nothing. As Harry's sniffling and tears increased, the judge passed him a box of tissues. *I'd have thrown it at him*, Kate thought, disgusted at his "poor me" antics.

Their two-year-long divorce proceedings had only deepened Harry's bitterness. He wasn't going down without a fight, and when his first two attorneys had urged him to settle, he hired a third. Whether the third time was the charm or his female attorney was overly charming, Kate wasn't sure. She only knew that thousands of dollars later, they finally reached an agreement.

The drawn-out trial had worn Kate down, mentally and physically. She was two dress sizes smaller. Although she was happy with her weight loss, it had come at great expense. She'd lost her husband and her two grown children weren't speaking to her, thanks to Harry's contagious animosity.

Having survived being left out of Anne's wedding, Kate was surprised when Mark invited her to his and Carla's. She thought it a step towards healing the family and she appreciated being included. With Mark's upcoming nuptials to reality star wannabe Carla, Kate believed things could only get better. She was unprepared for Harry's rehearsal dinner toast saying the Johnson family would soon be whole as Jamie was moving back into their family home with Kate. Kate was seething that Harry would make an announcement so far from the truth. The truth was she had been included in the wedding festivities because Harry wanted a platform to embarrass her.

Jamie had laughed at the suggestion. The longer they'd lived away from him, the more she'd fought with Kate over visiting Harry.

"I don't like going out with him. He creeps me out. Always patting my knee, trying to give me hugs. You need to tell him I don't want to see him," Jamie told Kate over and over again.

"He's your father. He loves you. I'm not telling him that; it'll only hurt him." And, she'd wanted to add, he'd accuse her of driving a wedge between them. Instead, she said, "In the words of Betty O'Brien, 'Buck up, buckaroo.'"

Although Jamie eventually stopped complaining about visiting Harry, Kate suspected she wasn't any happier about it. She'd started snapping at Kate and talking back to her.

"You need to stop sassing me. I'm your mother. It isn't nice, and that's not like you," Kate told her after she'd questioned Jamie's computer time.

Jamie looked at Kate, turned, and walked away. Quietly, but just loud enough so Kate would hear, she mumbled, "I'm your mother; it's not nice," in whiny imitation of Kate. Kate was infuriated but didn't know what to do.

What she did do was what she'd done in the past. She turned to Harry for help.

"I haven't seen that side of her at all," Harry said when Kate called. "She's fine with me. Maybe it's you. You need to be more patient."

What I need to be is smarter, Kate thought after she hung up. It was the same ole Harry—no help, just blame.

"Anne and Mark are trying to get Jamie to move back with Harry," Kate told Molly as they met for their weekly walk at the park. It was a brisk but sunny day, and Kate hoped the walk and good weather would lift her spirits.

"They say it's where they're a family," she added as

they passed the two-mile marker.

Molly took a few deep breaths. "You're her family, too."

"I don't live in that house anymore, so as Mark pointed out, I'm not part of the family. It's like they are trying to erase me from their lives, and Harry's leading the charge. He's redecorated the whole house."

"Not surprising. Harry's always fancied himself some sort of interior designer. Plus, how many times has he redone the patio and backyard? It's nutty."

"I know, but I'm afraid it's working. What will I do without Jamie? I've already lost Anne and Mark, and they're determined to take Jamie away from me. Jamie just showed me a new cell phone Harry bought her. Only he and the kids have the number. They call her at all hours of the day or night."

"Wow. That's so wrong. Talked to Harry about it?"

"Yep. He says she needs privacy and claims I monitor her calls. Says I'm trying to keep her away from her siblings."

"Jamie's smart. She has to see it for what it is."

"I hope so, but it's the two other kids and Harry against me. They're like a cult. I can't compete with designer clothes, trips to Europe, and the promise of a new car and puppy."

"What? No pony?" Molly asked.

"The pony could be next," Kate answered solemnly. "And he's sending her letters. So are Anne and Mark."

"Saying what?"

"No idea. She reads them and hides them."

"Have you asked her about them?"

"Yeah, she says it's no big deal. They're just saying hi

157

and being nice. It's the same ole, same ole. Harry's always believed in writing letters. Thinks it adds to his legacy. Guess Mark and Anne are doing the same thing."

Molly knew Harry had obviously put on a full court press, and Kate was headed for the sidelines. If Jamie moved back with Harry, Kate would have little chance of getting her back. Their relationship would be destroyed. She wished she could assure Kate that, in the end, Jamie would choose to live with her, but she knew that would be giving Kate false hope. Maybe the best thing a friend could do was just listen, and when the time came, try to figure out how to console her.

Three weeks later, Jamie told Kate she'd be spending more time at her dad's. Kate was dumbfounded, even though some part of her had known this was coming. Jamie's assurance, "It'll just be for longer weekends," did nothing to calm her fears. She knew Harry and how persuasive he could be.

Trembling, keenly aware of the knot in her throat, Kate asked, "Why?"

"Come on, Mom," Jamie shot back. "It's not like you and I are getting along. You're constantly correcting me, telling me how 'sassy' I've become. You even asked dad about it."

A bolt of anger and fear shot through Kate. Harry was using her words against her. She never should have asked him about Jamie's smart mouth. Hoping to right her wrong, Kate walked over to Jamie and put her arm around her. "Love you so much, sweet Jamie. You helped me get through the divorce. We've had our ups and downs, but most mothers and teenage daughters do, so—"

"Yeah, yeah," Jamie interrupted her as she pulled away. "Whatever it is, I need a break. Kind of like what you said you needed from Dad, right?" Her voice dripped with sarcasm.

Shocked by Jamie's terse response, Kate stepped back and raised her hand. Jamie looked at her, wild-eyed. "What? Going to slap some sense into me? Tried that on Dad, didn't you? You're crazy. Dangerous. I'm calling Dad," she yelled. Grabbing her coat, she ran out the door.

Where had Jamie's sudden anger come from? *I should have never forced her to spend time with Harry,* Kate thought. *I set myself up.*

Confused and worried, Kate was even more concerned about how it would play out with Harry. She looked for her phone, deciding she'd better call him before Jamie blew their argument out of proportion. Where was her phone? After five minutes, she determined it was among the missing. Time to say a prayer to St. Anthony.

Minutes later, it dawned on her; she'd left it in the car. After a short thank-you to the saint of lost things, she went out to the car and found her phone. Punching in Harry's number, she was concerned he wouldn't answer. He rarely answered her calls and called her back only when it was convenient for him. By the time Kate's call connected, Harry had already spoken to Jamie.

"What the hell's going on?" he yelled without even saying hello. "Going to beat Jamie into submission? You're out of control. Stop drinking the wine. Get yourself some help. Jamie isn't safe with you."

"She's perfectly safe with me. You know damn well I wasn't going to slap her," Kate said, exasperated. "Jamie knows that too. She's just working it and—"

"You've slapped me. I won't let you abuse Jamie like you abused me. This is going to stop, right now. She's moving back home, where she belongs," Harry barked. Then he hung up.

Kate was horrified. She had raised her hand to signal Jamie to stop giving her lip. She'd even stepped back from her. She was angry, but she'd never intended to strike her. Kate had never hit any of the children and had no intention of starting. How could Jamie not have known that? Harry had clearly known it as well. He knew Jamie could be dramatic, especially when she wanted her own way. She'd been like that since she was a baby.

Kate called Harry back. The call went to voicemail. Frantically, she tried Jamie's cell.

Jamie didn't answer.

This is just a big misunderstanding, Kate told herself. But she felt cornered. Scared. They were implying she was an abuser. Harry had even reminded her that she'd hit him in the past. As embarrassing as her lack of self-control had been, Harry was an adult, an emotional abuser. He'd deserved the slap and more. Jamie was an impertinent child, *her* impertinent child, not her lying, cheating husband. Her hand flew to her mouth as if to shut out her thoughts. Harry would use this to get Jamie to move back home. Her breath caught in her throat and she slumped into a chair. Would Jamie shut her out, too?

Her mind a jumble of thoughts and her emotions in overdrive, Kate began crying softly. She tried calling Harry and Jamie over and over again but got the same result. She needed to talk to someone, get someone to help her straighten things out. She didn't trust herself or her emotions, so she called her sister. When Sue answered, Kate began to sob.

"What's wrong? Kate, talk to me. What's happening?"

"Harry..."

"Has he hurt you? Are you in danger? I'll be there in ten minutes."

"No, wait," Kate responded between gulps of air. "I'm okay, just need to talk. I can't believe what's happening."

Two minutes later, after Kate had rehashed the ugly confrontation, she was able to stem her sobbing.

"Everyone's overreacting," Sue said. "Harry knows you weren't going to hit Jamie; he's just trying to get to you. It's his life's work. After Jamie calms down and spends a day or two with Harry, she'll get over it. She's a drama queen, like most teenagers."

"What if she doesn't get over it?" Kate asked. "What will I do if she moves in with Harry? I love her so much; she's all I have. He can't really take her from me, can he?"

Sue believed if Harry wanted Jamie back home, he'd get her. She didn't want to believe Jamie would turn her back on Kate, but she knew Anne and Mark were putting pressure on her to do just that. They wanted whatever their father wanted and were determined to help him get it. Kate was expendable. She'd left the family. If they had to lie and destroy their mother in the process, so be it. It was, as Kate had once said, the three of them against her. Jamie was the holdout.

Before Sue could find the right words, Kate blurted

out, "Why is God letting this happen?"

Having no good answer and no direct line to the Almighty, Sue tried soothing things over by reassuring Kate this too would pass, though she had a hard time believing it. But all she wanted at that moment was to mollify Kate and give herself some time to figure out how to respond if Jamie actually did move in with Harry. Kate had told her Jamie had been mouthing off and playing mother against father, but Sue had thought it was just part of Jamie's growing process. If she were wrong, Kate would be devastated.

Two days later, Harry's attorney sent Kate a registered letter informing her that Harry was prepared to take her to court unless she agreed to let Jamie live with him. She read and reread the letter, not wanting to believe it was possible. Harry was trying to take Jamie away. Why was Jamie going along with it? It was just a mother-daughter spat.

Her first instinct was to fight back, but she knew Harry had deep pockets. He'd spend months fighting it out, and she'd spend thousands of dollars that she didn't have. In the end, she knew she'd lose not only Jamie, but also the ability to care for herself financially.

Torn between financial concerns and holding on to her daughter, Kate called her own attorney.

"Can't tell you what to do, but after working with you two years ago on the divorce, I think I know you pretty well. I believe you had no intention of hurting Jamie. You're a kind and caring mom."

Kate thanked him for his support and suggested he call

Harry's attorney and work things out before they were all dragged back into court. "I can't let him take her away from me. She's everything to me; I love her with all my good heart."

Sensing the desperation and pain in Kate's voice, the attorney offered, "I understand. I'll do my best."

If he didn't, Kate was prepared to ask his female colleague to step in. The woman had worked on their divorce proceedings, and Kate felt she might better understand a mother's anguish. Thinking she had options in her fight for Jamie, her hopes were dashed when the attorney called back.

"Spoke with Harry's attorney, and he claims Harry's in the hospital. He had some sort of incident."

"What do you mean?"

"He got dizzy and disorientated at work. They think he might have suffered a small stroke."

"Is he expected to be okay?"

"I suppose so. His attorney said he's coming home tomorrow, but the doctors want him to take it easy, avoid any stressful situations."

"Meaning?"

"Meaning we have to postpone litigation until he's cleared by the doctor."

"Jamie should move back in with me. He can't take care of her if he's ill."

"Well, the thing is," he started. Then he paused, searching for the least painful way to say what he had to say. "Jamie signed an affidavit saying she feels safer living with her father. We'd have to get the court to agree to hear our case. She'd have to testify."

Kate felt as if someone had punched her in the gut.

Despite being scared to death that she'd lose her daughter, she didn't hesitate to say "I don't want to put Jamie through a court hearing. I can't do that to her."

"Harry wins again," she whispered to herself.

Reluctantly, and with a heavy heart, Kate surrendered. Harry recovered and Jamie moved in with him. Kate went back to therapy.

Chapter Twenty-Five

Whether it's the icemaker dropping cubes, the furnace cycling on and off, or the windows creaking in the wind, the nocturnal sounds of a home can be unnerving. Kate was hearing them all and imagining worse.

She'd hoped that after Jamie moved out, she'd eventually get used to living on her own, but after a month of what-ifs and then-whats, Kate was exhausted. Her lack of sleep was making her short-tempered. Her internal devil reared its ugly head when Jamie visited.

"I see you got a few new things, painted the kitchen," Jamie said as she sauntered into the condo. "A lot of neutrals," she added, inspecting the kitchen and family room. "You need more color. Brighter pillows on the couch, a small floral chair for that empty corner." It was a suggestion, but it sounded like a demand.

Nervous she'd say something wrong, Kate smiled and nodded. Her relationship with Jamie was better than her relationship with Anne and Mark, but not by much. She desperately wanted to grab Jamie and give her a big hug, but she knew she'd end up sobbing, and Jamie would tell Harry that Kate had attacked her, so she refrained.

Kate followed Jamie as she walked down the hall toward her old bedroom. When Jamie stepped into her old room, Kate was puzzled. Was she having second thoughts about moving out, or was she looking for something? Before Kate could ask, Jamie spun around. "One of the twins is missing."

It took Kate a moment to remember that her daughter had twin dolls named Lilly and Lou.

"Lilly or Lou?" Kate asked.

"Lilly. Got Lou. They were packed away together, so..."

"I know, I always thought it was very sweet you were so concerned they stay together."

"I was like ten years old, too old to be playing with dolls. So, where's Lilly?"

"No idea. All of your things went to your dad's. I swear I'm not holding her hostage," Kate said with the slightest smile.

Jamie didn't notice the smile as she looked around her old room. Kate thought it looked sterile and uninviting without Jamie's colorful posters and teenage mess. These days she couldn't pass the room without breaking down in tears. She had tried keeping the door closed, and when that hadn't worked, she'd considered moving. But Jamie might come back, and Kate wanted things to be just as she'd left them.

Jamie stood transfixed in the doorway. Wanting to break the silence, Kate joked, "You can check the closet and look under the bed if—"

"Don't be ridiculous," Jamie said. As she turned around

to leave the room, she was inches away from Kate.

Kate stepped back and whispered, "Love you so much and miss you every day." A flash of anger crossed Jamie's face. She shoved her hair behind her ears, raised her chin, and breezed by Kate.

"You need to get it together. Say you're sorry and move back home where you belong."

"I have it together. Always have. Problem is, your father—"

"Don't want to hear it." With her hands over her ears, she spun back around. "Stop blaming Dad. You were the one who left. Did you forget you were the one crying and carrying on all the time?"

"No, not for one moment. There was a reason. I loved your father, always will. Just like I love you and Anne and Mark."

"Enough!" Jamie screamed, stomping her foot. "I shouldn't have come. You never change. I'm leaving. Sorry to upset you." She flung open the front door, her face contorted in anger.

"I'm not upset. Why won't you give me a chance?" Kate pleaded. "How 'bout we sit and have a glass of wine?"

"The balm of alcohol? Always works for you. Not me. I don't want to hear any more of your lies!"

One door slam and three profanities later, Jamie was gone. Kate wanted to rush out the door after her, but knew Jamie would run to Harry with a story far from the truth.

Proud she hadn't run after Jamie, but angry at herself because she had pleaded with her, Kate walked into the kitchen. Trying to find safety in routine, she made herself dinner. Nothing tasted right and she ended up dumping her salad in the garbage and her fish down the disposal.

She felt miserable, and turned on the news. Like her life, it was depressing.

She turned off the TV and tried reading the latest thriller on her iPad. Three chapters in, she decided the book had too many characters and so many unnecessary details it was giving her a headache. She popped two aspirins and walked to the bathroom to take a shower. Fifteen minutes later, she was tucked into bed.

The following night Kate woke up around three a.m., heard nothing, and went back to sleep. The next few nights were the same.

Confident she'd conquered her nighttime fears, she was caught off guard when she woke up at 3:30 a.m. to the smell of cigarette smoke. Having once been a smoker, Kate knew cigarette smoke permeated your clothes and hair.

Thinking she must have been near someone smoking and the fumes had wafted from her hair to her pillow, she switched pillows. When that didn't work, she threw back her covers and got out of bed to look outside. Opening the blinds, she saw that the yard was dark, but the moon was full. Nothing looked out of place. The deck table and chairs were just as she had left them. No telltale glow from the end of a lit cigarette.

Still smelling the smoke, she closed the blinds and moved across the room to look out the front window. Her front yard and the street beyond were deserted. Breathing a sigh of relief, she went back into her bedroom to retrieve her phone.

She powered it on as she crept out to the kitchen

searching for the source of the smell. Maybe she'd left a candle burning. The candle was unlit. Crossing the room, she caught a glimpse of something pass in front of the French doors. She jumped back and dropped her phone.

Dear God, Kate thought, *this is the terrifying part of the horror movie where I have to close my eyes. I don't want to see the face on the other side of the glass.* Stooping to pick up her phone, she caught a glimpse of the alarm panel.

The light was red. The system was armed. She left the kitchen light on, turned, and walked back to her bedroom. Passing by Jamie's old room, she stopped and peered in just to be sure the smell wasn't emanating from there. When she flipped on the ceiling light, she was greeted by a wave of nostalgia and the faint smell of Jamie's perfume. Would she ever get over the sadness of losing her daughter? Of losing Anne and Mark?

She turned off the light and closed the door, dragging herself and her memories of Jamie back into her bedroom. Kate locked the bedroom door and went back to bed.

The next morning, Kate attributed the smell to a crazy dream. She got out of bed, brushed her teeth, and dressed. She picked up the paper from the front porch and sat down with her coffee at the kitchen table. Opening the metro section, she was greeted by a picture of a smiling Harry in his latest Press Agents ad. He was wearing the orange tie and striped shirt she'd given him years ago for his birthday. *Ha, there were a few good things I did,* she thought as she pushed the paper aside.

After she'd straightened up the family room and put

in a load of laundry, she went to the grocery store. It wasn't a task she'd ever enjoyed, and buying food for only one person made it worse. She breezed through the store, and while waiting in line at the checkout, looked down at her vibrating phone. Seeing her sister's number, she decided she'd call her back from the car.

"How's it going living on your own?" Sue asked her after a quick hello.

"Okay. Still getting used to the sounds of the house."

"Never were the bravest soul. Mom's still surprised you're okay on your own."

"Speaking of mom, how is she doing?"

"Says she's feeling dizzy and run-down, but it may be the new heart medicine. Doctor said it might make her fatigued."

"Might just take some time for her system to adjust. I'll give her a call later."

"Any progress on the kid front?"

"Nothing much. Jamie came over but left in a huff. I'm thinking I'll invite them all over for dinner. Maybe make Mom's strawberry pie."

"Good plan. Who can resist Betty's pie?

Kate hung up and drove home. Going back over her conversation with her sister, she wondered why she still loved Harry and hoped things would change. He'd belittled her, betrayed her, and taken away her kids. Was she stuck in that fairy-tale life Sue and she had laughed about years ago?

Turning the corner onto her street, she was surprised to see her garage door open. Had she forgotten to check it when she'd left? After pulling in, she parked and scanned the garage. Nothing looked disturbed. After getting out of the car, she fiddled with the door's electronic eyes and made a mental note to recheck it before leaving the next day.

After unloading her groceries, Kate devoured a small salad, poured herself a glass of wine, and went in to start the shower.

Knowing it took a while for the water to get hot, she left it running and walked back to retrieve her wine. When she returned, steam was pouring out of the shower stall.

I was only gone a few seconds. How'd it get so hot so fast? she wondered. *Must have cranked the hot water all the way up.* Putting a towel around her hand, she opened the shower door and reached in. The faucet handle was red hot, but it was only halfway to its warmest setting.

It was unusual, but she regulated the temperature, took a shower, and got into her pajamas. Before setting the alarm, she decided to go into the garage to check the water heater.

Turning on the garage light, she walked over to the hot water heater. It looked as if it was working properly. Bending down, she studied the temperature dial. The red knob was turned to the hottest setting.

How'd that happen? She readjusted the setting, locked the garage door, and returned to bed.

Two nights later, just before four a.m., Kate woke to the same cigarette smell. She sprang up, listened for any unusual sounds, then got out of bed and edged over to the window. No glowing cigarette, no one lurking in the shadows.

Wanting to get to the source of the odor, she picked up her phone turned on the flashlight and walked to the kitchen. The oven and microwave were turned off and looked fine. Satisfied they weren't harboring a smoldering fire, she mumbled, "What the hell's going on?"

Not sure what else to do, she turned to go back to bed. A muffled thud stopped her cold. It sounded like it was coming from the deck.

She turned around, turned on the outside lights, and looked out at the deck. Nothing out there but an overturned deck chair. A gust of wind from the approaching storm, she reasoned. But as her imagination got the better of her, she thought, *This is like a really bad scary movie. In the middle of a dark stormy night, the woman hears something, sees nothing, and goes back to bed. Two scenes later, she's a dead, bloody mess.*

I'm not going down without a fight, she told herself as she pulled a knife from the kitchen drawer. She left the deck light on, rechecked the alarm, and, holding the knife at her side, ran to her room. *Just my luck, I'd fall on the knife and stab myself to death,* she thought, laying it on the nightstand. She locked the bedroom door, plugged in her phone, and got under the covers. Ten minutes later, she was fast asleep.

Chapter Twenty-Six

The next day, Kate and her sister met for lunch at the Branding Iron. The bowling alley/restaurant had been a family favorite when they were kids. Their parents liked the charbroiled steaks, and Kate and Sue liked the attached bowling alley.

"Can't believe we're back here. Place is just the same, still serving the donut holes instead of bread. Genius," Kate said, almost drooling as they waited for a table.

"I wouldn't know, you scarfed up the entire bowl of donut holes. Left the rest of us with crumbs," Sue recalled.

"Wah, wah. Your story touches my heart," Kate said, invoking one of their mother's famous retorts.

"You sound just like Mom," Sue said with a pained look on her face.

"Wish she were here," Kate said as they sat down.

Betty O'Brien had died two months back, and her loss hit the family extremely hard. What they thought was an operation to clear up a kidney issue turned into a death sentence. Ten days after the surgery, having never regained consciousness, Betty slipped away. Both girls could barely speak of her without tearing up. For Kate, the memory was even more painful because Harry, Anne and Mark came only to the wake. Harry had said he and the kids were too busy at work to attend the funeral mass. Jamie was there for both and Kate was forever grateful for her support.

Looking over at Sue, she said, "I need to tell you what's been happening."

Kate launched into a detailed description of the odd goings-on at her house. Sue listened and got wide-eyed, but said nothing.

"Think I've gone off the deep end?" asked Kate.

"No, wouldn't say that," Sue said.

"What would you say?"

Choosing her words carefully, Sue said, "It's odd, but maybe your imagination's getting the better of you. The cigarette smell could be a neighbor sneaking out for a late-night smoke."

"At three or four in the morning?

"Might be the way the wind is blowing. This isn't *The X-Files*. You aren't dealing with the smoking man."

"Well, someone is out there smoking. What about the garage door being open?"

"When we were kids, the garage door opened when Dad shaved."

"The days of a morning shave opening a garage door are long gone."

Taking one more stab at reason, she added, "The water

heater setting is odd, but come on—who'd want to spook you?"

"Don't know. Getting so I hate going to bed."

"You always were afraid of the dark and the part of the basement behind the furnace."

"I was a kid. That was my imagination. This is real. You don't think Harry's behind it, do you? Trying to make me insane? Like in that old *Gaslight* movie where Charles Boyer tried to drive Ingrid Bergman mad."

"That was just a movie. And Boyer had killed her aunt and was trying to cover it up. Harry's not a killer; he's a serial cheater, busy looking for the flavor of the month."

"You're right," Kate said, embarrassed she'd brought it up. Just when she thought she'd put Harry behind her, he was back. She needed to work on that.

Voicing her concerns made Kate feel a bit better. They finished their meal, and when they got up to leave Kate gave Sue a quick hug.

"Thanks for listening."

"Of course. Relax, stop reading those murder mysteries."

Sue was right. She needed to get a grip. Buoyed by thoughts of taking charge and overcoming her fears, she drove home. As she turned into her driveway, she saw the garage door was closed. Just as she'd left it. *Things are looking up*, she thought, waiting for the door to open.

But as she pulled in, she noticed that the backyard gate was open. Kate parked, got out of the car, and walked out to the gate. Maybe one of the neighbors' kids had left it open after retrieving their ball, she reasoned as she walked into the backyard.

Glancing over at her bedroom window, she spotted something white in the grass. Walking over, she saw it was a cigarette butt. That's why she had smelled the smoke. Someone was watching her. Panicked, she ran back through the open gate and into her car. She locked the doors and called her sister.

"Someone's been watching me," Kate said between gasps. "Gate was open. Cigarette butts under my bedroom window, on the deck. Garage door was down when I—"

"Are you okay? Where are you, Kate?"

"In my car. In the garage."

"Take a breath. Stay on the phone. I'm sending Pete over with our neighbor Jeff. Maybe you should call the police."

"What'll they do?" Kate yelled. "I haven't seen anyone. Nothing is missing. They'll have me committed!"

"Okay, didn't mean to upset you."

"You didn't. Someone else is."

Sue stayed on the phone until the men arrived.

"I'm sure there's nothing to worry about," Pete said as Kate got out of the car. "I'll check inside and have Jeff go around to the backyard."

Kate opened the door to the house and turned off the alarm. She followed Pete through the house and as they came back to the kitchen, Jeff came up behind her. Startled, Kate grabbed a small frying pan off the counter and swung around.

Jeff jumped back. "Hold it, slugger. It's only me."

"Your first line of defense is an omelet pan?" Pete said in amazement.

Kate looked down at the pan with an embarrassed

laugh. "I'm just so jumpy. Sorry, Jeff."

"I understand," he said, giving her a small pat on the arm.

"I did see the butts, but could your landscaper have left them?"

"Doubtful, they don't have time for a smoke. They're in and out in record time," Kate mumbled.

He smiled and Pete put his arm around her. As they walked to the door he suggested, "Get motion-detector lights in the backyard. Put your mind at ease."

Kate thanked them, said goodbye, and reset the alarm. She ran down the hall to her bedroom and locked the door. This time, she skipped the shower. No sense tempting fate.

Kate had motion-sensor lights installed on the garage and house. As an added precaution, she had the locks changed.

"I've no idea if the previous owner gave keys to other people. I know she was single, but she might have had an ex-partner or husband," Kate told Molly when they met for a bike ride. Power-walking was getting hard on Kate's knees, so they had switched to biking.

"You really think your things that go bump in the night have something to do with the previous owner?"

"Yeah. My neighbor Marilyn said she rarely saw her. Couldn't pick her out of a lineup. Maybe she had a spurned lover who doesn't know she moved. Maybe I look like her."

The more she thought about it, the more she convinced herself it had something to do with the former owner. Time to call the realtor.

"Got to do a little research. Still planning on getting

together for dinner next week?"

"If you're still alive," Molly said with a laugh.

When Kate called the realtor for information about the previous owner, she got a terse, "You know I can't give you background information on the seller. Privacy issue. Try looking her up."

Pesky privacy issues meant she'd have to do her own investigating. When she'd asked her elderly neighbors about the former owner, they'd said they thought she had dark hair, but had little else to offer. Kate thanked them and, determined to know more, Googled the woman. She discovered she worked for a local consulting firm. She had an MBA from Marquette University, was on the board of the local hospital, volunteered at the food bank, and "was proud to be able to work with the Boys and Girls Club." *Wonder if she's working on curing cancer*, Kate almost said out loud before correcting herself for her pettiness.

Undeterred, Kate moved to check her social media accounts. Nothing. Getting any more information would cost her. Didn't seem worth shelling out $19.95. *Now I'm the stalker*, she thought as she shut down her computer.

That evening Kate binge-watched four episodes of *Longmire* and scarfed down a small frozen pizza. She was hooked on the crime drama series and wondered why she hadn't married a nice, law-abiding moral man like Walt Longmire. She'd thought she'd done that when she married Harry, yet here she was unhappy and alone.

Maybe everyone had a happiness quota, and once it

was used up, that was it. Had she used up hers in her years with Harry and her three children? The possibility was overwhelming and made her wonder if she was just marking time until death. Her therapist called it depression, but Kate believed it could be her reality.

Realizing her trip down memory lane was depressing her even more, Kate tried to put her past and herself to rest. She went to her room, changed into her pajamas, and padded out to the kitchen for a bottle of water. Passing Jamie's old room, she stopped and flicked on the light. Tears came to her eyes.

Dragging herself away from the room and the painful memories, she walked down the hall, past the living room windows. She spotted something out of the corner of her eye. Stopping to wipe her tears for a clearer view, she saw a small sedan parked across the street. *Probably smooching teenagers*, she thought as she walked back to her bedroom.

Three hours later, she was wide awake. After tossing and turning for what seemed like an eternity, she got up and went to the family room for her iPad. She located her tablet and turned off the light. Looking across at the front window, she noticed the same car was still parked across the street. As she crept forward to the window, the car started up and pulled away. Relieved the car had moved on, she rechecked the alarm and went back to bed with her book. A half hour later, the book had worked its magic. She was sound asleep.

"How's life in your haunted house?" Molly asked Kate when she called to check on her the next day.

"House isn't haunted. Someone's haunting me."

"You said you ruled out Mother Teresa who once lived in your unit, so now who?"

Before Kate could answer, Molly cut in with, "Think a little retail therapy is in order. Get your mind off things. How about we meet at Nordstrom?"

Never one to turn down a little shopping expedition, Kate quickly agreed and left for the mall.

As the two friends rode up the escalator to the women's section, Kate found herself laughing at one of Molly's stories about her kids. Confident Molly embellished her stories for hysterical effect, Kate still enjoyed each and every tale.

Walking over to a rack with blouses, Molly pulled out a white shirt and handed it to Kate. Looking it over, Kate smiled. "I don't always wear white shirts. I have a few striped ones too. I'm even thinking of giving into the plaid fad."

"Wow. Your life has changed!"

"Somewhat," Kate said as she walked to the register. Turning back to Molly, she added, "And, I'm starting to think Harry may be behind what's been happening. Took away my kids, now he's trying to take away my sanity. My sister said that's crazy, he's too busy looking for the next young thing."

"My brother Mike ran into Harry and some Kellie woman at the movies," Molly said. "Mike wasn't impressed. Said she had a wet fish handshake and personality to match."

"I know her. She works for him. At least he didn't trade

up."

"How could he? He's been to the mountaintop..."

Kate let out a short snorty laugh. "Seen the Promised Land, but it wasn't enough."

"What's ever enough for Harry? He's never satisfied."

"Wasn't always the case. Money and success changed him. I keep hoping he'll come to his senses, be the Harry I fell in love with."

"You'd go back? Have you forgotten the three years of hotel bills your attorney found? How he wrote you those letters and told you they were for massages, no sex involved? You were devastated. In bed for two days till I came and made you get up and shower. I thought you'd have to be hospitalized."

Looking back on those days made Kate shudder. Why did Harry need to write her those letters—was it some kind of catharsis? Did he really think she was dumb enough to think he was at the Red Roof Inn and Hilton Garden for spa services? Just more excuses for his bad behavior.

"Still hard to believe Harry would put that down in writing. He really is way too sure of himself."

"He knows I'd never show it to the kids. I can't win. I can accept that my marriage didn't work out, but I can't accept losing my children. It's getting worse as time goes on," Kate said.

"They don't return my calls or texts. I keep thinking I'll run into one of them someplace." Putting her arm around Kate's shoulder, Molly said, "So sorry for all you're going through. I truly believe they will someday see the light. You're a good mom. Deep down, they know that."

"I wish they'd see that Harry isn't perfect," Kate said.

"You don't shoot the conductor when you're riding the

gravy train."

Kate knew it was true, but it still hurt. The children were half her, but they'd become nothing like her. Nothing like the kind, empathetic children she thought she'd raised, and she was powerless to change it.

"Thanks for listening to me complain."

"Anytime," Molly answered. Shifting her tone, she added, "Almost forgot to tell you, Bill and I are looking at a house in your development. Need more room and a bigger yard."

"Closer to me?"

"Close to you."

"Double points. Seals and Crofts or The Carpenters. Lost my husband and kids, but not my gaming skills," Kate declared.

Chapter Twenty-Seven

Driving home from yoga class, Kate spotted a gray sedan two cars back. The car followed her into her subdivision, and when she turned down her street, it came up behind her. Her stomach dropped. It looked like the same car she'd seen on her street in the middle of the night.

I am really letting this whole creepy feeling getting to me. There must be millions of gray cars like this out there. Plus, who would be dumb enough to watch me from the same car? Wouldn't you change cars?

Confident it was all a strange coincidence, she pulled into her driveway and opened the garage door. The sedan cruised by the house and out towards the main street.

Kate went in the house, took off her coat, and dropped her keys on the kitchen counter. Everything looked the same, but something didn't feel right.

When she walked into the family room, she noticed the chair near the bookcase was at an odd angle. The throw, normally on the back of the chair, was on the floor. When she went to pick up the blanket, something caught her eye. As she moved closer to the bookcase for a better look, she gasped. It was her wedding album, sitting on the fourth shelf next to Jamie's baby book.

She'd left it at Harry's when she'd moved out. She never wanted to see it again. She pulled it out from between two books and half expected to see her face x-ed out on the cover. It hadn't been. She quickly paged through the album and found no missing pictures or crossed-out faces. Confused, she had a frightening thought. Someone must have been in her house. Harry? How had he gotten in? Did he have her alarm code? Maybe he gave the album to someone else who had consequently broken into the house. One of the kids?

Snatching her phone from her pocket, she called her sister with her latest "Harry's out to drive me mad" installment. Sue listened, and after a short pause and a few hmms, said, "Take a step back, Kate. Think of what you're saying. Harry either broke into your house or had someone else do it. Then, he or they disarmed your alarm and put your wedding album in a bookcase filled with books? You might not have noticed it for months. Why would he do that?"

"Because he'll never get over the fact that I left. He'd delight in driving me slowly insane."

Sue hesitated, "Anything else out of place? Look around and I'll stay on the phone with you."

"Okay, I'm going into my bedroom and bathroom. Nothing's out of place. Jamie's room is still the same, and now that I'm back in the kitchen...let me check the knife drawer."

Sue let out a short giggle. "Surely he wouldn't cut off your head with your own carving knife."

"À la the three blind mice and the farmer's wife? Not remotely funny."

"Sorry, just trying to lighten you up. I'm sure there's a logical explanation. Ease up on the wine; it's killing your brain cells."

"And with that piece of sisterly advice, I'm off to bed," Kate snapped as she hung up.

This is getting crazy, and it needs to stop, Kate said to herself, as she got ready for bed. Worried what the night might bring, she went into the kitchen for a Diet Coke. As she opened the can, she knew it was time. She had to call Harry.

He picked up on the second ring. Kate was momentarily mute, as Harry never answered her calls. She always had to leave a message. "Oh, Harry," she began as she recovered. Then, in as calm a voice as she could muster, she went on to tell him about the smoke smells, garage door incidents, and wedding album. He listened and said nothing.

"Still there? Did I lose you?" Kate said, exasperated at his lack of response.

"I'm still here," Harry said, and paused before adding, "What do you want me to do? It's upsetting, but..." About to go on, he was hit with a revelation. "You think I'm doing it. That's crazy. You're losing it, Kate. Go back to your shrink. Get some help," he hollered as he hung up.

Why did I bother calling? What was I thinking? That he'd care that I'm terrified? He's the same ole asshole.

As angry as she was, she managed to get a few hours' sleep before her phone rang at four a.m. Fearing the worst, she bolted out of bed and fumbled for her phone. Had something happened with her parents or one of the kids? Was Harry calling back with round two? After four hellos, no one answered. She ended the call and checked the number. Unknown caller.

When Kate woke up the next morning, she vaguely remembered a middle-of-the-night phone call. Not sure it wasn't a dream, she checked her phone. Someone had called. No caller ID. It was strange and unnerving; all her nightly oddities happened in the three to four a.m. hour. Her mom called it the witching hour. Had something to do with ancient canonical hours of the Catholic Church. No prayers were offered during that hour, making it prime time for evil forces. Maybe she should call a priest, get an exorcism.

Her thoughts drifted back to Harry. Still mad he had hung up on her, she was even angrier with herself for falling for him and his two pennies nonsense so many years ago.

The next day when she stepped outside to retrieve the newspaper, she noticed a gray sedan was parked two houses over. As she picked up the paper, the car pulled away. It looked like the same car she'd seen the last few days, but she wasn't sure and didn't care. She was tired of thinking about her crazy life.

She read the paper, got dressed, and drove to the local farmers market. Kate had read that eating healthier made for better mental health and wanted to give it a shot.

Browsing through the various stands, she bought handmade soap, olive oil, and two pepper plants. After she paid, she moved on to the vegetable stands, where she spotted a young woman in black yoga pants and a hoodie. She couldn't see her face, but judging from her height and streaked blonde hair in a messy bun, she felt sure it was Jamie. With a racing heart, Kate walked over to the woman.

"Jamie?" No response. Did she know it was Kate? Was she refusing to acknowledge her? Uncertain what to do, Kate was spared any further confusion when a young man holding a baby walked up to the woman. The woman turned around; Kate's heart sank. It wasn't Jamie.

Disappointed, but thankful she hadn't embarrassed herself by taking the woman's arm or saying anything more, she turned her attention to the fruits and vegetables. As she studied the apples, she realized she was not only disappointed, but also relieved. What would she have said, and how would Jamie have reacted? *Probably turn and run away*, she thought as she walked to her car.

She was juggling the bags searching for her keys, when she looked up and saw something on the hood of her car. She moved closer to get a better look and stopped to catch her breath. "This is insane," she said as she looked around the parking lot. Half expecting someone to pop up and say, "Yes, it is—and yes, you are." She started to shake. Setting the bags down on the pavement, she stood staring at the large bunch of daisies on her hood. They looked similar to the bunches displayed at one of the farm stands.

Now, here they were—but why were they there? Had someone placed them there as they had gotten into their car and forgotten to pick them up? That had happened at the grocery store once when someone left a six-pack of beer in an empty cart next to her car. A bit of Irish luck, she'd reasoned, as she'd put the beer in her car.

Could this be a random act of kindness she'd read about?

She looked for a card, but there wasn't one. *No sense leaving them here,* she thought as she picked up her grocery bags. A bunch of her favorite flowers on the hood of her car was odd, but most things in her life were odd now. *Might as well take them home and put them in water.*

After she got home, brought in her bags, and put the fruits and vegetables away, she contemplated calling Sue or Molly to tell them about the flowers. Maybe she could make a joke about having a secret admirer, but on second thought, she decided she'd better not. They'd probably have her committed. She was alone in whatever was happening. She stood in the kitchen, phone in hand, tears streaming down her face into the corners of her mouth before she even realized she was crying.

Kate had convinced herself there was nothing sinister about finding the flowers on the hood of her car, so she cut the stems and put them in her favorite vase. It was a blue-flowered vase Anne had given her on her birthday. She couldn't recall what birthday, but that didn't matter. What had mattered was she still had a small piece of Anne in her life.

Close to tears again, Kate's heart ached for her children. Reason had told her she wouldn't have survived if she had stayed with Harry, but at times like this, she wrestled with her decision to leave. She had believed leaving would be a wake-up call for Harry. She had convinced herself he would apologize for his bad behaviors and that after his display of contrition, she'd agree to work out things between them. That hadn't happened.

Harry had convinced himself and their children that Kate was off her rocker. Broken their hearts and embarrassed the family. He had been determined to make her pay for "abandoning the family." The family had become Harry and their three children, with Kate as the outsider. And she knew now he planned to keep it that way.

A week later the daisies had wilted, and only one more three a.m. hang-up call had disturbed Kate's sleep. Well-rested and more comfortable living alone, she was ready to try a new tact with her children. What she had done in the past hadn't worked. Her calls had gone unanswered and her texts and cards had been ignored. Last Christmas, Anne had returned the sweater Kate bought for her. No note, no explanation, just the pink cashmere sweater in its original box. Jamie hadn't sent her gifts back, but hadn't acknowledged that she'd received them. After three texts asking if they arrived, Kate got a "yep." Mark kept his checked shirt and crew-neck sweater, as she had known he would. She'd bought it at Harry's favorite men's store, and it was exactly what Harry would have worn. She never got a thank-you and never knew if he'd worn it. Knowing Mark's wife, Carla, Kate wouldn't have been surprised if she had re-boxed the sweater and regifted it to Harry.

Not wanting a repeat this year, Kate took a page out of Harry's playbook. She wrote each child an individual letter filled with funny stories and happy family memories. Each letter ended with an apology for any pain she had caused and a sincere hope for a better relationship. She had even suggested they meet for lunch or coffee as a first step. Satisfied with what she had written, she mailed the letters.

No one ever responded.

"I thought one of them, especially Jamie, would have texted. Even a thank-you, or a 'don't bother me again,' would have been something," Kate told Molly.

"Unbelievable," Molly said as she unpacked moving boxes. It had taken them a year, but Molly and her family had finally moved closer to Kate.

"You read about mothers who are drug addicts, burn their babies with cigarettes, or bring home strange men. Their children still love them," Kate said, pained to her core.

"Your kids love you. I remember how they'd call you multiple times when we met for lunch or shopping. Thought they were a little too dependent on you, but I never said anything. This is all Harry. He's done the same thing to them that you said his mom did to him and his brothers when their dad left. Made them choose one parent or the other."

"My shrink called it parental alienation. Psychological abuse where one parent deliberately isolates the kids from the other parent. Read a book about it. It said there's realistic estrangement, where a parent's abusive behavior or substance abuse is behind it, or pathological alienation, which isn't a rational response to the behavior of the alienated. I'd say I'm experiencing the latter."

"I'd just call it evil. Terrible thing for a parent to do. Make kids choose Mom or Dad."

About to comment, Kate was interrupted as Molly's three kids came bursting in the door from school. Happy to see Kate, they gave her a quick hug before bounding into the kitchen for after-school snacks. Kate remembered when her own kids were that young and happy to come home to her. Seemed like a lifetime ago.

"There's fruit gummies and chips in the cabinet on the right. Let me finish unpacking this box and I'll see what else I have," Molly yelled after them. "You'd think they were starving Armenians."

Kate had to laugh, even though she realized now it wasn't all that funny; her mom had said the same thing.

"When I was a kid, I always wondered," she said, "if the Armenians were really starving. Made me sad."

"They were. Yes. Result of the 1915–1930 Armenian genocide."

"'Don't know much about history, don't know much biology,'" Molly sang back. "1960, Sam Cooke. A King of Soul classic."

"On that note, I'm off," Kate said as she stood up to leave.

"To see the wizard?" Molly shot back.

"Yes," Kate laughed, "the wonderful Wizard of Oz."

"Did you know Dorothy's original slippers were silver? They were changed to ruby for Technicolor."

"No, I didn't, but I see you've expanded into movie trivia."

"Trying to level our playing field."

"How kind of you," Kate said as she walked to the door. Kate was happy Molly and her family had moved closer to her, but seeing her friend with her loving children hurt. Kate missed her own children more and more each day.

191

She wondered if she'd end up like Anne had once said she would, "a lonely old lady with no family."

Driving home from Molly's, Kate was overcome with nostalgia when she heard the same song that she'd heard when she'd met Harry. It had been decades ago, but she could still smell the rich aroma of freshly brewed coffee that had wafted through the small, warm shop where she and Harry first met. She could almost see herself studying at the small table near the window, watching kids play in the snow. In the midst of it all was Harry, the good-looking senior who had charmed her with his "two pennies for your thoughts" line.

Felt just like yesterday, but that was three kids ago and a lot of hurt. What had gone so wrong? Why had he cheated? Why hadn't she seen it sooner? Had Marcy been the first? As she wrestled with an answer, her sister's words came back to her.

"This is on him. Cheated just like his dad. Must have forgotten how it hurts."

She knew Sue was right, but their dad's old saying, "Fool me once, shame on you; fool me twice, shame on me," haunted her. Harry had fooled her time and time again. The more she thought about it, the more she'd wished she'd shot him and gotten it over with. Lucky for Harry, they didn't own a gun. Then again, if they had, he could have shot her, and with his luck, gotten away with it.

Deep in thought, Kate failed to see the car make a turn in front of her. The driver hit his horn and Kate hit the brakes. Her car stopped inches from a small white car.

Shaken but grateful she'd avoided an accident, she held her hand up as an apology. The other driver rolled down his window, gave her the finger, yelled "Crazy bitch," and sped off.

"Fuck you, asshole!" Kate yelled out after him. *Not smart*, she thought after she'd said it. Her mom had always warned her, "Often a person's mouth breaks his nose." She'd laughed at the Irish proverb, but knew in her heart it was true.

Stop overthinking this, she told herself as she turned onto her street. She brushed aside the incident and pulled into her garage. She got out of the car, walked to the door of her house, and unlocked it. Still lost in thought, she turned back around to close the garage door. The fact that her house alarm hadn't sounded didn't occur to her until she stepped into the kitchen to turn on a light. Momentarily confused, and a bit nervous, her eyes darted around the room. Nothing looked different or out of place. She laughed nervously, trying to convince herself that she must not have set the alarm before she'd left. *Another thing I need to pay better attention to*, she told herself as she put her purse down on the counter.

That's when she saw them. She took in a large gulp of air and cried out, "Dear God!" And God must have heard her, because he immediately transformed her into a pillar of salt, just like Lot's wife. She couldn't move. She felt sick to her stomach.

It seemed impossible, but yet here they were. Perfectly placed side by side on the kitchen counter were two shiny Lincoln pennies.

Chapter Twenty-Eight

Three days later, taking a deep breath, swallowing her gum, and smoothing her hair, Kate followed Mark into Harry's hospital room. Anne and her husband, Joe, were sitting alongside Harry's bed. Still a blonde, blue-eyed beauty, she presented her classic style: a white shirt, black pants, pearls, and nude pumps. She always looked neat and put together, and today was no exception. Anne looked up, said nothing, and returned to thumbing through her magazine.

Her husband Joe, an average-looking guy with dark hair, dark eyes, and a trace of day-old stubble, mirrored her look, but without the pearls and pumps. Joe, who'd always been kind to Kate, glanced up from his phone and mouthed a silent hello. Joe was easygoing and liked to keep the peace. Harry said he was wishy-washy, as he rarely talked politics or expressed his opinions on world affairs. Kate thought him smart and wise.

So far, things are going just swell, Kate thought as she

turned her attention to the patient. No doubt it was Harry lying there, but it wasn't the Harry she remembered. This Harry was much thinner and seemed smaller than his once strong six-foot frame. Surrounded by beeping monitors and two IV drips, he looked like the poster child for a bad medical show. His hands and arms were brown with age spots, and the gray hospital gown was a far cry from his standard button-down shirts and crew-neck sweaters. Kate was struck by the fact that he looked like any sick old guy.

Harry, however, had never been just any old guy. Kate thought about the way he'd always worn clothes from top designers and had made it a point to look his best. How he favored bold ties, tasseled loafers, and light socks, Dave Letterman style. He'd rarely worn jeans and had only one ratty T-shirt. He'd owned two tuxedos, a closet full of French-cuffed shirts, and three cashmere topcoats.

Taking pride in his personal and professional appearances, he had never smoked, eaten too much, or laughed too loudly. Harry enjoyed a cocktail or two, and had also been happy to polish off a good bottle of wine, especially with his childhood friend Bishop George.

A dirty joke never left Harry's lips, and he'd rarely sworn because he thought it reflected a lack of self-control. His mother had referred to him as the kid who wouldn't say shit even if his mouth were full of it.

Harry was a walking advertisement for his Press Agents billboards and bus cards, which declared "If you want to look better and go farther, you need go no farther than the closest Press Agents."

Looking down at him, Kate couldn't help but wonder if this bed was as far as he would go. Was he, as her father often said in his later years, "on his final exam"? Maybe it was sad that he might meet his maker before sixty, but she couldn't help feeling he was getting what he deserved. It made her heart just a little bit lighter to know there really was such a thing as karma, and it was biting him in the ass.

Lost in thought, Kate was startled when Anne stood and announced, "They gave him a mild sedative a few hours ago so he should be coming to pretty soon. Been here awhile though, so now that you're here I'm taking a break."

Kate stepped back and stammered, "Of course. I'll be here if he wakes up. If something changes, I'll text."

Anne turned, and without looking at Kate, walked out of the room. Her husband obediently followed, but gave Kate's hand a small squeeze as he left.

Chapter Twenty-Nine

Harry was gradually waking up. His head moved side to side as he struggled to stay awake. His eyelids fluttered open and he took some deep breaths in an attempt to clear his head. He had heard just voices before, but now all he heard was incessant beeping. He hated repetitive noises and someone needed to make it stop. His eyes darted around the room and his heart skipped a beat as he focused in on the figure approaching his bed.

Dear God, it's Kate? Wasn't she here before?

Momentarily confused and unsure if he was thinking straight, Harry honed in on Kate.

Bet she's trying to play the good ex-wife. Hoping to get her kids back? Never happen...she deserted them. Abandoned us. I've been there for them; I've taken care of them.

The more he thought about it, the more he convinced himself Kate was there just to stir things up.

Wonder who told her? Can't believe the kids would.

Maybe George called her.

Now, wide-eyed with anger, he watched her slowly pull a chair to the side of his bed. The pillow that Anne had used to ease her aching back when she sat in the same chair was in Kate's hands.

She's going to smother me. She's the one who put me here. Going to finish the job. I need someone to help me. Save me from Kate.

She wasn't sure if she wanted to talk to or choke Harry. Looking at the pillow she held, she quickly put it back on the chair. She hated him and a pillow to the face wouldn't change that.

As she glanced back at the machines keeping him alive, she was once again reminded of her mother's death. She still remembered the pain on her father's face as he stood watching the life drain out of his life partner. Saddened by the thought, she turned her attention back to the man who was once the love of her life.

"You're a horrible human being," she said as she slowly moved closer to his face. Leaning over him, she raised her hand over his head.

Harry's eyes were bulging from their sockets and his heart was pounding in his chest. A small cough came from his throat as he tried to lift his arm.

"Ah, I knew you could hear me. Scared I'll send you to dry-cleaning heaven?" she said as her hand came down and simply brushed his hair off his forehead.

"Made you a little nervous, hmm? More nervous than you made me? You've been gaslighting me. It wasn't enough that you took my children from me, you tried to rob me of my sanity."

Harry blinked and opened and closed his fist.

"That a yes?" Kate hovered closer to him. "I'm over you, but I'll never be over you turning my kids against me. That is unforgivable. Worse than a mortal sin."

And, Kate thought, *you can't talk, which means you can't go to confession. Get absolution.* It made her smile as she leaned back and whispered, "You will rot in hell."

Moving away from the bed, Kate turned to walk towards the door. As she brushed by one of the machines, she stopped and looked up at the bags of fluids keeping Harry alive. She touched one of the lines as her other hand dropped two pennies on the tray table over his bed. He let out a short gasp and grunted.

She smiled and in the stillness was reminded of something Ingrid Bergman had said in the movie *Gaslight*:

"I'm rejoicing in my heart, without a shred of pity, without a shred of regret, watching you go with glory in my heart!

About Atmosphere Press

Atmosphere Press is an independent, full-service publisher for excellent books in all genres and for all audiences. Learn more about what we do at atmospherepress.com.

We encourage you to check out some of Atmosphere's latest releases, which are available at Amazon.com and via order from your local bookstore:

Relatively Painless, short stories by Dylan Brody
Nate's New Age, a novel by Michael Hanson
The Size of the Moon, a novel by E.J. Michaels
The Red Castle, a novel by Noah Verhoeff
American Genes, a novel by Kirby Nielsen
Newer Testaments, a novel by Philip Brunetti
All Things in Time, a novel by Sue Buyer
Hobson's Mischief, a novel by Caitlin Decatur
The Black-Marketer's Daughter, a novel by Suman Mallick
The Farthing Quest, a novel by Casey Bruce
This Side of Babylon, a novel by James Stoia
Within the Gray, a novel by Jenna Ashlyn
Where No Man Pursueth, a novel by Micheal E. Jimerson
Here's Waldo, a novel by Nick Olson
Tales of Little Egypt, a historical novel by James Gilbert
For a Better Life, a novel by Julia Reid Galosy
Big Man Small Europe, poetry by Tristan Niskanen
The Hidden Life, a novel by Robert Castle
Big Beasts, a novel by Patrick Scott
Nothing to Get Nostalgic About, a novel by Eddie Brophy
Whose Mary Kate, a novel by Jane Leclere Doyle

About the Author

A former newspaper reporter, columnist, and editor in Cleveland, Ohio, Eleanor is a Chicago native who now resides in Atlanta, Georgia. *A Pressing Affair* is her first novel.

CPSIA information can be obtained
at www.ICGtesting.com
Printed in the USA
BVHW031705300421
606209BV00007B/878